"We found her boat floating free of its anchor in Quincy Bay. And we located a piece of her clothing that looks like an animal, possibly a shark, had ripped to shreds."

"But you haven't found her body."

Detective Rafferty shoved the note into a manila envelope marked EVIDENCE, yanked open the drawer to his left, and dropped the missive inside.

"I wish I could help you, Miss Alexander. I really do. The case will remain under investigation, but unfortunately, there are too many real criminals on the prowl for me to waste time and manpower figuring out why Lydia Alexander took her life. Your aunt is gone, dead by her own hand. How or why is something we may never know." His gravel-laced voice softened. "Go home. See to your aunt's things. Make whatever arrangements you need to bring closure, and then move on."

Don't miss out on a single one of our great mysteries. Contact us at the following address for information on our newest releases and club information:

Heartsong Presents—MYSTERIES! Readers' Service
PO Box 721
Uhrichsville, OH 44683
Web site: www.heartsongmysteries.com

Or for faster action, call 1-740-922-7280.

Where the Truth Lies

Elizabeth Ludwig and Janelle Mowery

HEARTSONG
PRESENTS
MYSTERIES

To our families.
We love you all.

ISBN 978-1-59789-530-9

Scripture taken from the HOLY BIBLE, NEW INTERNATIONAL VERSION®. NIV®. Copyright © 1973, 1978, 1984 by International Bible Society. Used by permission of Zondervan. All rights reserved.

All of the characters and events in this book are fictitious. Any resemblance to actual persons, living or dead, or to actual events is purely coincidental.

Cover Design: Kirk DouPonce, DogEared Design
Cover Illustration: Jody Williams

Our mission is to publish and distribute inspirational products offering exceptional value and biblical encouragement to the masses.

Printed in the U.S.A.

1

"Suicide!"

Casey Alexander stared across the coffee-stained desk at the Pine Mills detective peering down his nose at her. "That's not what the police in Virginia Beach told me. They said you contacted them with news she was missing. They didn't say anything about suicide."

"We didn't have all the information at that point. That's why I needed to speak with you, confirm some of her activities. Unfortunately, our investigation has turned up a few, shall I say, details, which make me believe it's more than just a missing person case."

"Look, Detective. . ." She glanced at the name etched on the bronze plate. "Rafferty. Aunt Liddy is many things—zany, eccentric, you name it. But she's not unstable, nor is she suicidal. You'd need some pretty serious evidence to make me think otherwise."

Eyebrows raised, Detective William Rafferty lowered his head to peer over his reading glasses. Without a word, he slid a rumpled scrap of paper sealed inside a plastic bag across the desk.

Casey stole a quick glance at Aunt Liddy's familiar writing. It was too horrible to believe. She shoved the bag back. "Aunt Liddy would never take her own life. You've made a mistake."

The detective's gaze hardened, and the knuckles of his interlocked fingers whitened. "Our office isn't in the habit of making mistakes, Miss Alexander. I realize this is a shock. No one wants to believe someone they love could be so desperate."

Casey shook her head, both palms waving aside his suggestion. "You have to at least consider the possibility that Aunt Liddy was murdered."

He lifted the note and held the signature side toward her. "Is this your aunt's handwriting?"

Aunt Liddy's scriptlike scrawl flowed across the page. She swallowed past the burning lump in her throat and nodded.

"Our handwriting analyst came to the same conclusion." He lowered the paper and handed her an envelope. "I made a copy for you in case you wanted to read it in private."

Casey stuffed the letter into her purse next to her ever-present pad of Post-it Notes. "Is there anything else?"

"We found her boat floating free of its anchor in Quincy Bay. And we located a piece of her clothing that looks like an animal, possibly a shark, had ripped to shreds."

"But you haven't found her body."

Detective Rafferty shoved the note into a manila envelope marked EVIDENCE, yanked open the drawer to his left, and dropped the missive inside.

"I wish I could help you, Miss Alexander. I really do. The case will remain under investigation, but unfortunately, there are too many real criminals on the prowl for me to waste time and manpower figuring out why Lydia Alexander took her life. Your aunt is gone, dead by her own hand. How or why is something we may never know." His gravel-laced voice softened. "Go home. See to your aunt's things. Make whatever arrangements you need to bring closure, and then move on."

"What about this?" She snatched her purse off the floor and pulled out a small cardboard box. "Aunt Liddy sent it to me a week before she died."

She peeled back several layers of tissue paper to reveal the mottled silver key nestled inside.

Detective Rafferty lifted the key, balancing it between his thumb and index finger. "What's it for?"

"I don't know. Aunt Liddy's letter just told me to hold on to it."

"That's a little vague, don't you think? Kinda fits in with my theory that she wasn't in her right mind."

Casey dug her nails into her palms. She hated to agree with him, but he was right. It was a little weird. "Maybe, but I still think it's important."

Detective Rafferty pushed back from the desk. His swivel chair creaked like a rickety porch swing on a windy day. With his hands folded across his ample belly, his rumpled gray suit, and a striped tie complete with jelly stains, he looked like every police lieutenant on every cop show Casey had ever seen.

"Have you been to the post office or the bank? Maybe it fits a lockbox."

"Not yet, but I intend to do that as soon as I leave here."

After a long moment of silence, Detective Rafferty leaned forward, slid the key toward her, and rested his arms on the desk. "Can I give you some advice?"

Casey clamped her lips shut in mutinous defiance. Did he really expect her to answer that?

"Let this go," he continued without waiting for her response. "Your aunt was a nice lady. I liked her. She deserves to rest in peace."

Casey reached for the key and dropped it back into its box. Her hands shook with anger, and tears clouded her eyes. She loved Aunt Liddy, and she would not let this farce of an investigation tarnish her reputation. "I agree, Detective, and I'm going to do everything in my power to see she does just that."

She rose. Detective Rafferty beckoned to a tall, brown-haired officer hovering outside the door. "Brockman, would you kindly see Miss Alexander to her car?"

With a stiff nod to Detective Rafferty, Casey headed for the exit. Not waiting for his junior sidekick, she strode out of the station, down the stairs to the sidewalk.

"Hey, wait up! Miss Alexander, please. Wait."

She spun on her heel, fuming. "Look, Officer Brockman, if you think I'm going to listen to one more bad word about Aunt Liddy—"

He hurried forward, hand outstretched. Between his fingers he clenched a small white business card.

"I just wanted to say that I knew Lydia. Liked her a lot. In fact, she used to cut my hair."

Casey studied the earnest-looking officer. So he was a customer of Aunt Liddy's. Hesitantly, she took the card from his fingers.

He glanced over his shoulder toward the station. "I don't know what happened to your aunt. Wish I did. I can understand your wanting the details. If you find anything. . .if I can help in any way, give me a call." He tipped his head toward the card. "Okay?"

She nodded cautiously. "Thank you." His concern appeared genuine, unlike the detective, but she was still leery of the offer, since Rafferty had already told her they wouldn't spend a lot of time investigating.

He gave a half smile then turned and went back inside.

Casey sighed. The brick facade of the Pine Mills Police

Department sneered down at her, its many windows grinning like some giant, toothy jack-o'-lantern.

Go home? Get closure? Was Rafferty kidding?

The strap of her leather handbag dug into her arm. She jerked it over her shoulder. She'd just learned that Aunt Liddy was missing and presumed dead. The last thing she intended to do was leave this backwater hole-in-the-wall before she found out exactly what she wanted to know—why.

She rubbed at the tears pooling in her eyes and followed the peony-lined sidewalk toward the silver BMW parked next to the station. Detective Rafferty might not like it, but she would open her own investigation with help from the police or no. She hadn't spent countless hours reading about Brandy Purcell's adventures in the True Life Detective series for nothing.

"Casey? Casey Alexander?"

She paused with her fingers curled around the door handle. A tall, barrel-chested man, cheeks reddened and hair swaying in the crisp spring breeze, hurried across the street toward her. He sported a brown leather cap, and reflective sunglasses hid his eyes. The defense mechanism that came with living in a large city kicked in. She fumbled with her keys, instinctively searching for the biggest, thickest one she could find. She'd read once that it was possible to thwart an attacker using them.

"Yes?"

The man drew to a halt a few feet shy of her passenger door. "I'm Jack Kerrigan. Remember me? I was a friend of Lydia's."

It took a moment for recognition to snap. "Jack? Jack!" She dropped the keys back into her bag and hurried around the car. He shifted the rolls of white paper under his arm and enfolded her in a hug.

Jack Kerrigan looked as though he belonged on the cover of a Wheaties box. Casey remembered him working out, jogging regularly. Even at fiftysomething, he had a body college grads would envy. She drew back, surprised by the tension she felt in him.

"How—how are you?"

He chuckled and tapped the rolls of paper. "Oh, business is crazy. I just got back from a meeting with our architect. You?"

Though it had been several years since she last saw him, the change in Jack's appearance was remarkable. Gray streaked the raven hair, and lines crisscrossed his weathered face. He looked pale, drawn. . .tired.

She swallowed. "Oh, I've been better. Just finished up with Detective Rafferty."

He glanced at the police station. "Was he helpful?"

Her sunglasses poked from the top of her purse. She pulled them out, shined the lenses on her pant leg, and slid them on. Her composure once more intact, she shrugged and turned her back on the building. "Not so much, but no matter. I'll find what I need without them."

"Liddy was a dear friend, Casey. I'd like to help, if I can." He followed her around to the driver's side.

Casey allowed him to open the door. "Okay. I'll give you a call—"

He cut short her words with a wave. "Why don't I stop by late this afternoon? You'll be staying at your aunt's place, I assume?"

"I'm headed there eventually. I've got some stops to make first."

Jack's interest dissipated faster than a light fog on a

warm day. He glanced over his shoulder while he waited for her to climb into the car. Once she sat inside, he closed the door and patted the roof.

"See you later." He whirled and headed across the street the way he'd come.

Casey started the engine and hit the power button to lower her window. "Sure, Jack. It was nice to see you again. Can't wait to catch up." Her words poured out faster, louder, as he walked away.

She blew out a deep breath, put the car in gear, and drove the four blocks to the Pine Mills Savings Bank. Along the way, she passed the Ice Creamery, cheerful and inviting with its brightly painted roof and antique windows. Casey gulped back a sob. Aunt Liddy had taken her there often. Sometimes they made up reasons to go. She could still taste the chocolate melting on her tongue. She sped up and focused on the large building at the end of the street.

Like the rest of the town, the bank wore its age proudly. Red, white, and blue bunting fluttered from the windows. Pathways decorated with flowers wound around the front and stopped at the steps, which were flanked on both sides by tall white columns. Casey parked, lifted the key from its box, and went inside.

Huge. Cavernous. Even if she tried for days, she'd never come up with a word that did the place justice. She could put on lipstick by her reflection on the gleaming marble floors. She adjusted her scarf and blazer, smoothed the wrinkles from her matching slacks and silk blouse, and walked past the red velvet rope line toward a row of glassed offices.

"Okay, thanks, Jeff," said a young brunette.

"No problem, Monah. Let me know if that key gives you any trouble."

Key?

Casey stopped and backed up to peer through one of the open office doors. Sure enough, "Monah" held up a silver key similar to the one clenched in her hand. With a final farewell, Monah got up, left the office, and headed toward the service desk.

"Excuse me," Casey said, darting in front of her.

Monah tucked a white bank envelope into the tiny macramé purse bouncing on her hip. "Yes?"

"I know this will sound strange"—Casey opened her hand to reveal the key lying flat on her palm—"but does the key they just gave you look anything like this one?"

The young woman looked taken aback. She glanced first over one shoulder, then the other. "Um. . .I don't think I caught your name."

No wonder she looks like a doe in the headlights, Casey thought. *I might as well have bowled her over and ripped the key from her purse.*

"I'm sorry." She pulled back her hand with a sheepish grin. "I'm a little overzealous at the moment. My name is Casey Alexander. I'm Lydia Alexander's niece."

"Lydia's niece!" Monah's eyes widened behind her preppy black spectacles. "I hoped I'd get to meet you. She's told me so much about you."

Dull grief tightened Casey's stomach. "Thanks. Listen, I was wondering—"

To her surprise, Monah took her arm and led her to a quiet corner of the bank. Potted palms hid them from prying eyes. Nestled among the plants were two brocade-covered chairs. Monah sat on one, Casey on the other, close by.

Monah put her hand to her chest. "My name is

Monah Trenary. Did Lydia ever mention me?"

Casey shook her head. "I don't think so. Should she have?"

The hopeful light in Monah's eyes faded. Surprised by her fervor, Casey unclasped her hands and touched Monah's elbow. "It's been several months since I spoke to her. I've been swamped getting my Web design business off the ground. Maybe she did, and I forgot."

Monah twisted a strand of her long brown hair between her fingers. "Well, it's just that Lydia and I got to be friends after she started coming to the library. We talked a lot, about God and stuff. Matter of fact, she accepted Christ not more than three months ago. That's why I find it so hard to believe—"

She broke off and grasped one of Casey's hands. "You don't believe she committed suicide, do you? Not Lydia."

"Aunt Liddy. . .Aunt Liddy talked to you about God?" Casey blinked, trying to process all Monah said in one simple sentence.

"Yeah, and she was more full of spunk than ever. Do *you* think she was ready to end her life?"

Finally, someone who thinks like me. Casey shook her head so hard her hoop earrings bumped against her cheeks. "No, I don't. The woman I know never would have acted so selfishly. But I can't for the life of me think why anyone would want to do her harm."

"Maybe that's where I can help, if you'll let me. Not that I think Lydia had enemies, mind you, but I've lived here all my life, and I know just about everyone. Maybe I can answer your questions."

Optimism curbed by caution over her new ally swirled in Casey's stomach. She bit one corner of her lip and nodded. "Okay, then maybe you can tell me about this. Aunt Liddy sent it to me."

She retrieved Lydia's key. This time, Monah didn't shy away but pulled out her own key and held the two side by side. It was obvious they didn't match. Casey stifled a stab of disappointment.

"Sorry," Monah said. "She didn't tell you what it's for?"

"No, but I'm just getting started. I'm headed to the post office next, and then Aunt Liddy's house. Something will turn up."

Monah glanced at her watch. "Wish I could go with you, but I'm due at the library in less than an hour." She tore a piece off the bank envelope, scribbled a couple of phone numbers across it, and handed it to Casey. "Call me if you need anything. I wrote the library's phone number on there, too, just in case." She rose, her long hair swaying. "I'm glad you're here, Casey. Maybe now the police will have to do something. They wouldn't listen to me."

Casey offered a wry smile. The police hadn't listened to her, either, but it was a comfort to know someone else had tried. "Thanks, Monah. I'll call you."

Monah left, taking her green tea scent with her. Casey folded the paper and slid it into the pocket of her billfold. She decided to check her voice mail before heading to the post office. A message from her secretary told her that one of her clients accepted the Web design she'd proposed before leaving Virginia Beach for Pine Mills, Massachusetts. At least something was going right.

She remembered the location of the post office without much trouble. She'd accompanied her aunt on more than one occasion to buy stamps. Outside, a line wound from the double glass doors down the sidewalk.

What in the world?

Purse in hand, she exited the car and went to take her place in line.

"Hello there."

Casey turned to look at the kind face that accompanied the friendly voice. "Hello."

"Gotta love tax time." The woman, easily in her late fifties or early sixties, held up a long white envelope. "Are you mailing your return?"

Tax time. Casey grimaced. She still hadn't gotten hers filed. "No, ma'am." She peered around the line of last-minute filers at the doors. From here, the sunlight bouncing off the glassed entrance winked like a lighthouse.

"Did your filing early, huh? I always tell Delbert we wait too long. I wish he'd listen to me and get this silly thing taken care of in January." She waved at the people standing in front of her. "Seems like the line gets longer every year."

"No kidding." The words sounded harsher than she'd intended. She took off her glasses and poked out her hand. "I'm Casey Alexander."

The woman smiled, revealing two rows of perfect dentures. The flowered scarf wrapped around her pink foam rollers snapped and fluttered in the breeze. She put up her hand to stop it from flying off.

"I'm Ethel Dunn. You say your name's Alexander? I don't suppose you're Lydia's niece?"

Several heads turned to stare, and no wonder. The woman practically shouted to be heard above the wind and voices.

"Yes, that's right," Casey said.

The old lady nodded, her head bobbing like a yo-yo on a short string. "I thought so. Lydia talks on and on about how much you and she look alike." She tapped the fingers of her right hand against her bottom lip. "I'm surprised to see you. A planned visit?"

Obviously, the news of Aunt Liddy's demise wasn't public knowledge, and Casey wasn't in a hurry to change that. "Not exactly." She tipped her head to peek toward the doors.

Ethel patted her arm. "She's so proud of you. If ever there was a person who loves her niece, it's Lydia."

Casey glanced around at the growing number of interested bystanders. "Thank you," she said, cutting her off before the speech got longer. "Maybe we can catch up another time?"

She slipped out of line, ignoring the irritated looks tossed her way, and wound toward the entrance where a female postal worker stood directing people to available windows.

"Sorry, ma'am. I'm afraid you'll have to wait your turn."

Casey tugged the key out of her purse. "Yes, ma'am. I've just one quick question. This doesn't happen to look familiar, does it? Maybe a post office box?"

The postal worker barely glanced at it. "Nope. Ours are bigger and have fatter heads. Plus, there's an ID number on them for when we have to reorder." She reached around her and waved to the next person in line.

Panic gripped Casey's insides. "I'm really sorry." She dipped back into the woman's line of sight. "I know you're busy. But could you look again just to be sure? It's very important."

The lady took the key in one hand and gestured people forward with the other. "See right here?" She pointed with a chubby, brightly painted finger. "It should say 'United States Postal Service' or 'USPS.' It's not ours."

"Oh."

Disheartened by the quick rejections that met her first attempts at tracking down a clue, Casey shoved the key back into her purse and walked, head lowered, to her car.

"Okay," Casey sighed, sliding onto the BMW's heated leather seat, "what would Brandy do?"

Star of the True Life Detective novel series, Brandy Purcell was Casey's favorite character. She flicked her long blond hair over her shoulder and tapped her temple the way Brandy always did whenever a case had her stumped.

"Think. Think. Think." Suddenly self-conscious, she jerked her finger from her temple and looked around. She had to stop copying a fictional character. People were bound to think she belonged in a nuthouse. She snapped her fingers. The house. The key was an important clue, no doubt, but surely there would be others. She started the engine and pointed her car toward the highway.

Aunt Liddy lived in an old Victorian two-story a few miles outside of town. Along the way, high stone walls carved from the belly of the Appalachians rose on each side. Wildflowers dotted the valleys, and with her window cracked to catch the crisp spring breeze, she could smell just a hint of pine.

The mountains had always fascinated Aunt Liddy, and Casey loved visiting them with her. Hard to imagine her gone.

She wiped her damp eyes and then adjusted the mirror to check her mascara. No streaks. Good. She lifted her hand to push the mirror back and paused. Funny. She hadn't seen any other cars earlier, but bearing down on her was a large black pickup. She slowed and eased over to let the vehicle pass. No good. The driver refused to budge. Up ahead, the road narrowed where it curved into the mountain. A deep chasm gaped on the opposite side.

She clenched the steering wheel tighter, her nervousness building. Behind her, the headlights in the rearview drew closer, looking like some ancient, angry gargoyle. She tore her gaze from the mirror.

Relax your grip. Accelerate into the turn. Don't oversteer.

Easy to say. The hundred-foot drop looming to her right made it difficult. She held her breath as one of the front tires rumbled off the road, spewing dirt and gravel. With a smooth, controlled jerk, she pulled the car back, knuckles white, legs shaking.

The yellow-eyed beast inched closer. Casey no longer saw the yawning grille in her mirror. It was too close and getting closer. The first thump nearly sent her skidding out of control. She quelled the urge to stomp on the brake and corrected the fishtail, pressing on the gas.

"God, help! Help me!"

Up ahead, a scenic turnout sloped up the mountain. If she could get that far before the truck hit her again. . .

She risked a peek. The black Chevy inched closer, its engine roaring as the driver downshifted. She couldn't slow down to make the turn. It was all or nothing.

She dropped her right hand to the parking brake and timed the turn. The truck hugged the centerline. He'd force her off the mountain with the next hit. She waited, heart pounding, as the turnout rushed to meet her.

The Chevy crashed into her bumper. The car's back end swung hard. The steering wheel jerked and would have ripped from her hand if she hadn't been ready. With the added momentum, she almost missed the turnout. She gasped as the edge of the mountain swirled by outside the window.

Once she hit the turnoff, Casey wrenched up on the parking brake. The back tires squealed as the car swung around, spitting smoke and gravel. She grabbed the wheel, tried to steer with the spin, and nearly threw up when at last the car rocked to a stop.

Her hands shook so badly, she fumbled for several seconds with the door handle. At last she kicked it wide and scrambled out of the car. She tripped, caught herself, scraping her palm in her haste to get away.

She headed for the tree line. Branches ripped across her face as she threw herself into the woods and squatted behind a scrubby bush. Above the sound of her own ragged panting, she strained to hear if anyone followed. After several moments, her breathing slowed, and the surroundings returned to their former stillness.

Whoever drove the truck must have sped away when I went off the road. They either thought they got me or gave up, she thought, shuddering.

She left the safety of the trees and crept toward the car. The soft idle of the engine mingled with the *ding, ding, ding* of the open door.

Thank God for those defensive driving classes she took last summer. She signed up after Brandy Purcell nearly got killed by an angry suspect in the latest book of the True Life Detective series, *Backward Glance.* Hands shaking, she reached inside the car and flipped off the key.

In the center console lay another pad of Post-it Notes and the pencils she'd bought after reading book

2, *Downward Spiral*. Brandy Purcell always had Post-it Notes handy to jot down clues. Casey thought it was a good idea.

She scribbled, "Late-model Chevy, black, extended cab," on a yellow sticky note and pressed it to the window.

"Hey there!"

Casey nearly jumped out of her skin. The voice rang off the rocky walls, echoing so she heard "Hey there!" over and over. She pulled her head out of the car. The late afternoon sun shone in her eyes, blinding her, but when she squinted, she saw a man running toward her with a shovel clenched in both hands.

Her breath caught. A muscular male wielding a shovel could really do some damage, and she didn't have Brandy's martial arts skills to fall back on.

2

His heart pounding to the beat of his stride, Luke Kerrigan raced down the sloping road toward the car sitting at an odd angle in the scenic turnout. The way the person leaned over the front seat, he wondered what he'd find.

Lord, let them be all right.

"Hey," he hollered again, this time drawing the person's attention. His steps slowed and then stopped altogether when a blond pulled herself from the car, yellow paper and a pencil clasped in her hands. She shaded her eyes against the sun, but he would've recognized that attractive figure anywhere. He grabbed his shovel with both hands and swallowed hard.

"Casey?" He walked the last few yards, dropped the tip of the shovel into the gravel, and reached for her. She jerked back, almost cowering. He frowned. "Are you okay? Did you get hurt?" He examined her from head to foot but saw no blood. Her blue eyes were dazed but not dilated. She looked good, in fact. Very good. He cleared his throat. "From where I was, it sounded like you stopped pretty fast."

"Um, yeah. I. . ." She waved toward the Appalachian Mountains in the distance. "I wanted to take some pictures." Luke glanced in the direction of her gesture. "Yeah, the view's great from here." He motioned toward her hands. "But wouldn't a camera work better?"

Casey looked down and then back at him, a grimace spreading across her face as she tossed the Post-it notepad and pencil onto her car seat. Luke ducked his head to see inside. Yellow notes papered her dash, making the front end look as if it had bloomed daisies. Lydia had told him about Casey's latest penchant. He would have teased her, but the tremor that ran through her made him bite his tongue.

"You sure you're all right?" He eyed the skid marks again. "A ride like that would have shaken anyone."

She ran her fingers through her wavy hair. "I'm fine. Really. Don't let me keep you."

Luke leaned on the shovel. "I'm in no hurry." He nodded toward the rear of her car. "I hope you're not either. You might want to forget the pictures and take care of that."

The car's tire sagged into the dirt. "Here." He stuck out his hand for the keys. She gasped and shrunk toward the car. Her gaze stayed fixed on the shovel like a cat's eyes on its next victim.

He frowned. "You do remember me, don't you? Luke Kerrigan. Lydia's friend." His heart thumped. "My condolences, by the way."

"Yes. Thank you."

He lifted the shovel to put it aside. She cringed. Time to get rid of the thing. It seemed to make her nervous. "Hang on a minute." He walked to the edge of the gravel, stomped the head of the shovel into the dirt, and returned. Luke stifled a smile at her look of surprise. At least she appeared more at ease. "As long as I'm here, I'll change your tire for you. Pop the trunk."

She moved to do as he asked, then stopped and frowned. "Why are you here, Luke?"

He did smile then. "Lydia, for one. You, for another."

"What do you mean?"

He leaned on the trunk. "I thought I saw you in town. I was headed out to Lydia's house to see if it really was you. Then I remembered the plants she told me about before she. . .well, before she died."

"Plants?"

"Yeah." He motioned up the road. "She said she saw some strange but pretty plants out here and thought I'd like to take a look."

"So you're not on foot?"

Luke cocked his head to the side. "No, my truck's parked up the way a little farther."

"Can I see it?"

"What? The plants or the truck?"

She rubbed her hand along her arm as if she were cold. "Uh. . .both."

He stared at her. She was serious. . .and acting rather strangely. But then, he didn't really know her all that well. The person he'd created in his mind came mostly from what Lydia had told him along with a few brief introductions at times when she'd visited town.

He shrugged. "Sure. Up this way."

They walked in silence for a while, with only the drone of a small engine plane flying overhead. Casey followed a couple of steps behind him. He had to turn back to talk to her. "How long are you staying?"

Her lips thinned. "As long as it takes."

Puzzled, he slowed so she could move alongside. "As long as what takes?"

"To find out what really happened to my aunt." The last word came out in a choking sound, and she stopped. "Is—is that your truck?"

"Yeah. I—"

Casey turned and sprinted back down the slope toward her car. Luke stared after her. She could break an ankle the way her high heels wobbled from side to side. She stopped flailing her arms long enough to jam her feet further into the shoes then continued on her way. Luke raced after her.

"Casey? Wait!" He caught up to her before she reached the car and grasped her arm. "What's wrong?"

She jerked away. "Nothing. I just—I remembered I need to be somewhere."

Nothing? Her eyes flickered in a wild dance as though fear itself gave chase. But why? He couldn't think of a thing he'd said or done that would put her in such a state. Maybe it was best to forgo any conversation and let her get going.

"All right. Let me help you fix that tire so you can be on your way." He headed toward the car.

"I can do it."

He gave her a once-over. "Really? You've changed a tire before?"

"Well, not exactly. But I've seen it done on TV."

Luke leaned against her car. "This I gotta see. If you were planning to use Post-it Notes to take pictures, I can't wait to see what you intend to use for a jack. What do you have? An extra pair of pumps in the trunk?"

The slightest twitch moved the corner of Casey's mouth, and Luke was certain she almost smiled. . .the first time since he saw her today. His hopes rose.

"All right. Let's get this trunk open." He moved to the back and waited while she unlocked the trunk. He removed her suitcases then flipped up the carpet, pulled out the spare, and leaned it against her car. "Whoa. What happened here?" He turned and looked at her. "Your bumper is all scraped and dented. Did you back into something?"

"Not exactly." She fidgeted and peeked inside the trunk. "What else?"

He grabbed the jack, placed it under the car, then removed his jacket and laid it on the ground so she wouldn't get too dirty.

The next several minutes passed in quiet explanations. Every time she leaned close, the scent of her perfume propelled Luke's senses into chaos. He didn't know what kind it was, but it sure smelled good. Then she pulled away, making him wonder if he smelled bad. A quick, unobtrusive sniff alleviated that fear. Maybe she just needed her space. He gave a mental shrug. The day he figured women out was the day he knew he'd died and gone to heaven.

Once he'd set the spare onto the hub, he placed and turned the nuts as she handed them to him. He ignored the face she made at the gunk clinging to her fingers. "You said something earlier about finding out what really happened to your aunt."

She glanced at him out of the corner of her eye. "Yes."

"Care to elaborate?"

"So you're like everyone else around here and believe she committed suicide?"

"I don't like to think so, but—"

She turned, her eyes glittering. "But what?"

Luke stopped to look at her. "Well, the last month or so, she started acting different."

She pushed aside some flyaway hair, leaving a smudge

on her face. "Different? How?"

"I don't know. It's hard to put a name to it, but I guess you could say she seemed a little nervous or tense."

"Do you know why?"

"No. I asked once if she was all right, and she said she was fine."

A small frown creased her eyebrows. "Interesting."

The change in Lydia had bothered him since the day he found out about her death. "So she never mentioned anything to you about something being wrong?"

Casey gave a slight shake of her head.

He hefted the tire iron, gave each nut one more hard turn, lowered the car, and tossed the old tire into the trunk along with the jack. Then he replaced the suitcases and slammed the trunk lid closed. "Take that to Bob's Garage. He'll get you fixed up. He can probably take care of that bumper for you, too."

"So I'm all set?"

He followed her to the driver's side door. "Yes. No, wait."

In his pocket, he carried several business cards. He patted his shirt for a pen. Nothing. He must have lost it while digging up the plants. He spotted the pencil on the seat and ducked inside for it. A sticky note caught his attention. *Late-model Chevy, black, extended cab.* Why was she describing his truck? He pulled out in a hurry, only to smack the back of his head on the door frame. He gritted his teeth.

"You okay?"

He gave the spot a quick rub. "Yeah. It's one of the prices I pay for being tall."

He jotted his home phone number on the card and

handed it to her. "If you ever need anything, Casey, anything at all, please call. All my numbers are there."

"All right. Thanks for your help." She slipped into the car.

"Sure. Anytime."

The door slammed closed at the same time the engine roared to life. In seconds, Luke stood alone, his thoughts as cloudy as the dust storm Casey left in her wake.

Casey stared into the rearview mirror, watching Luke disappear in a cloud of dust. Well, almost. He was built just like his father and too big to disappear completely. And handsome. She didn't remember him being so cute. . .or tanned. . .and he smelled good. She slammed on her brakes.

He smelled good? For crying out loud, Casey, the guy tried to run you off the road.

Or did he? Surely, if he'd wanted to harm her, a rusty shovel would have done the trick.

She wound down the mountain, passing by a quaint country church, with its tall white spire piercing the sky, and four old mills from which Pine Mills probably got its name.

Her fingers tapped the steering wheel. It had to be coincidence that she'd run into both Kerrigans on the same day and that Luke was on that deserted stretch of highway, driving a late-model, extended-cab black Chevy, digging up plants at exactly the same moment someone tried to run her off the road. Her throat went dry. Even in her head, the idea sounded ludicrous.

But he changed her tire. Why would he have bothered if he intended to do her harm?

Maybe because someone was watching?

She shuddered. Had there been traffic on the road after Luke walked up? Yes, come to think of it. And he hadn't offered to help right away.

But he was Aunt Liddy's friend. She spoke of him

often, and Casey even met him once. . .or twice. She shook her head. Okay, so she'd met him several times. So what? The murderer in *Death Watch* turned out to be Brandy Purcell's neighbor, and she'd known him for years. Better to be safe.

She started a mental list of possible suspects and added Luke's name next to coworkers, relatives, and former friends, all people she intended to check out, satisfied that as long as she investigated everyone, she'd cover all the bases.

At last the gingerbread-cutout gables of Aunt Liddy's house came into view. Casey parked in the driveway and stared up at her aunt's darkened bedroom window. It was the first time she could remember seeing it dark. Usually a candle stood sentinel, lighting the way home, Aunt Liddy often said.

Casey swung the car door open. Blooms transformed the dogwood tree. Flower buds dotted the hydrangea bushes, and the crab apples showed signs of erupting any moment. Soon the air would be heavy with the scent of flowers and cut grass.

At least the yard looked good. Great, in fact. She eyed the sidewalk in amazement. Aunt Liddy had been an avid gardener, but when had she put in all the new flower boxes? She pinched off a bloom, brought it to her nose, and climbed the steps to the front door. Prompted by her movement, the motion-sensing lights popped on, illuminating her way. Five days' worth of papers lay scattered across the porch. She'd pick them up after she had a chance to unpack. Speaking of which. . .

She unlocked the front door and propped it open so she could roll the suitcases inside. She turned on several lamps in the parlor, dropped her purse on the hall tree's oak seat, and went back for her bags.

Dusk gave way to night. Casey went down the steps and circled the car. Down the road, headlights rounded the corner and slowed to a stop in front of the house. Jack Kerrigan climbed out of his low-slung sports car, one hand raised in greeting, the other clutching a brown paper bag. The black sweater he wore made his gray hair appear all the more polished.

"Let me help you with that," he called as Casey popped the trunk and prepared to pull out her suitcase. He crossed the lawn in a few quick strides.

"Thanks, Jack. Be careful. It's. . .a little heavy."

"Yeah." Jack grunted as he twisted and tugged to yank the bag out of the trunk. At last he freed it, slid out the handle, waited while she retrieved the two smaller suitcases, and followed her up the walk. "Thank goodness this thing has wheels."

He parked the case in the hallway and held up the paper bag. "Hamburgers. I figured you didn't have time to stop for groceries this afternoon."

The scrumptious scent of pickles and fries wafting from the bag made Casey's stomach grumble. "You're right. I didn't, and that smells delicious. Thanks, Jack."

She led the way into the kitchen and found plates, cups, a two-liter bottle of soda, and the pearl-handled spoon Aunt Liddy used to stir her tea. Tears burned Casey's throat at the sight of it.

Jack came to stand behind her, his hand warm upon her shoulder. "You all right? You look like you've seen a. . . Never mind." He smiled in apology. "Sorry, Case. I can't get used to her being gone, either. I forget the idea is new to you. I've at least had a couple of days."

Casey swiped her hand over her eyes. "No, don't apologize. It's just weird is all. I'll be fine."

"Are you sure?" Jack touched her forehead. "What happened there?"

She rubbed her head, checked her hand, then peered at her reflection in the darkened window above the sink. "Oh, that. Flat tire. Give me a minute to clean up, would you?" She gestured to the table where Jack had their supper laid out. "Don't let that get cold. Go ahead and start without me."

She walked down the hall to the bathroom. Rose-dotted paper covered the walls. An antique light crowned the mirror. Lavender scented the towels. Everything reminded her of Aunt Liddy.

"So when did you get into town?"

"What?" She stuck her head out the door.

Jack leaned back in his chair, burger in hand. "I said, when did you get into town?"

She made one last pass over her face with the towel and slid it over the rack next to the washbasin.

"Late this morning." She flipped off the light and headed back toward the kitchen. The meal smelled delicious, but. . . "You don't suppose Aunt Liddy has olives, do you? I love olives on my hamburgers."

He jumped up, grabbed a jar from the fridge, and set it on the table next to the ketchup. "Here you go, kiddo."

Kiddo? Casey grimaced. Her dad used to call her that, when he wasn't working late at the shipyard.

Jack pulled two napkins from the pantry and handed one to her, keeping the other for himself.

"You sure know your way around a kitchen." She piled several olives on her plate and grinned. "Come here often?"

A flush stole over his cheeks and turned his ears red. "Yeah, well, old habits, and your aunt is. . .was a good cook."

The hum of the refrigerator filled the sudden silence. Casey took a bite so she wouldn't have to answer.

"Um. . .Casey, when you've finished, there's something I'd like to talk to you about."

She eyed him over the rim of her glass. "Okay."

He gathered up his plate and cup and deposited them in the sink. The wrappers he crumpled and threw in the trash. "Ah, it's about the house actually. I was just wondering if you've decided what to do with it yet."

"Not really." She shrugged. "I haven't had much time to think on it. Plus, we won't read the will until. . ." She paused, roping her emotions. "Until her case is closed. The house isn't really mine—"

Jack waved his hand. "That's just a formality. Lydia wanted everything to go to you. She told me many times."

He moved back to the table and sat, elbows propped and chin resting on his knuckles.

Casey pushed aside the remainder of her burger. Beneath the light of the Tiffany chandelier hanging over the table, Jack looked too old to be the friend she remembered Aunt Liddy having. He was taking her death hard. She covered his hands and gave them a squeeze. To her surprise, Jack grasped her fingers and held them tight.

"Casey, did Lydia ever tell you about me?"

She smiled. "Of course. You were a dear friend. She talked about you a lot."

He stared into her eyes and finally let go of her hands with a sigh. "Yeah, we were pretty close, which is why I want to help you."

"Help me? Then you don't think she committed suicide either?" Casey's words tumbled over themselves to get out. She jumped out of her chair, almost making it topple. "I'm so glad to hear that. I've been thinking. We should read her note—"

Jack stood with her. "Whoa, whoa. I meant help with the house. I figured I could help you get rid of it. Maybe buy it from you so you're not stuck here longer than you need to be. Besides, this place has kinda grown on me."

Stunned, her mouth hung open, and she stared at him in disbelief. "Get rid of the house?"

He spread his hands wide. "Well, what else are you gonna do with it? It's not like you can move here. What about your business?" He took her elbow and gestured to the table. "I'm sorry, Casey. I didn't mean to shock you, but you must've at least considered it. Let's sit awhile and talk it over."

She resisted the pull on her elbow and looked around the kitchen at the painted pine cupboards and lace curtains. This may not have been her house, but it was home. She shook her head. "No, actually, I haven't thought about anything but solving Aunt Liddy's murder."

This time, Jack's mouth fell open. "Murder! What on earth—?"

She retrieved her purse from the hall, pulled out the rumpled copy of Aunt Liddy's letter that Detective Rafferty had given her, and unfolded it. Behind her, Jack read out loud over her shoulder.

> *To all my family and friends,*
> *I know my death will come as a surprise,*
> *especially to those I love and who love me. But*

I've reached a point in my life where I could come up with no other solution. I know you won't understand, but trust that I know this was best.

Casey, I hope you will always remember the special times we shared at our favorite place along the river at the park. Visit it once in a while and think kindly of me. Continue to pursue your mysteries. I know they make you happy. I love you, dear girl.

I apologize for the pain I will cause so many of you. Do not mourn me, for I will be with you as long as I live in your hearts. Know that everything is in God's hands. I love you all dearly.

Lydia Alexander

She craned her neck to look at him. "Doesn't look like any suicide note I've ever seen."

Jack's brows rose as they resumed their seats. "How many have you seen?"

"Three."

"Three!"

"Well, they were in a book. Three books. Brandy Purcell's books. But they were all bestsellers." She was rambling. She quit talking and bit her bottom lip. Jack took the note and scanned the lines again. She waited until his head lifted, her hands clenched tightly in her lap. "What do you think?"

Jack took his time folding the note. He laid it on the table and looked at her, his blue eyes bright with compassion. "I think we both loved your aunt very much, and we're going to have a hard time letting go, but we will, because we have to. Have you thought about a memorial service? It'll help you get closure."

That made two times someone had told her she needed closure. Her teeth hurt from clenching them. She picked up the note and stuffed it back into her purse.

"Thanks, Jack. I appreciate your concern, but I'm not convinced that I need closure, not until I find out what really happened. Luke mentioned something about Aunt Liddy acting differently the last month or so, and I need to know why. But first I want to go to the park like she suggested, spend some time alone in our place."

To her surprise, his eyes narrowed. He let out a heavy sigh. "I wish I could change your mind. Things are going to be difficult enough without adding a dispute as to how she died. After all, we need to think about what she would have wanted."

Casey squared her shoulders and rose. She went to the door and stood with her hand on the knob. "I think she would have wanted me to listen to my heart. And right now, it's telling me that something doesn't feel right. Thanks for dinner, Jack." She swung open the door and tapped her foot, waiting.

Jack shook his head and rose, an imposing figure in his black turtleneck sweater and slacks.

Funny. He didn't look tired anymore. She held her breath as he stopped next to her and dipped his head to press a kiss to her cheek.

"Call me, kiddo. Let me know what you find out."

She nodded, closed the door behind him, and slid the dead bolt into place. The lock didn't compare to the alarm system at home, but at least she'd be able to sleep and dream about what she'd find in the morning.

4

Y̶ou don't want that tree there."

Luke stood next to his truck with Ranger Steve Agee and the chief groundskeeper, Ross Derkson. Honored that they'd asked his opinion on the needed face-lift at the state park's front entrance, Luke planned to give them something they'd be proud of.

"Why not?" Ross pointed at his drawing. "It's perfectly centered in front of the building."

"That's one of the reasons you don't want it there. How often do you see nature so centered and uniform?" Luke touched his finger about an inch away from where Ross had his. "I'd plant it right about here and put, say, a boulder or something like that on the other side. Then we fill in the rest of the area with shrubs, flowers, and a welcome sign. With the tree near the corner, you'll still get the shade you're looking for."

Steve nodded. "Sounds good to me."

A grunt rumbled from Ross as he leaned against the truck. "I don't know. What I drew looks pretty good."

Luke tried not to smile. "All right, consider this." He stepped to the area in front of the building where Ross wanted the tree planted and lifted his arms just above shoulder height. "Picture the tree here in a few years. I don't imagine anyone inside that booth will appreciate their view being blocked."

Tapping rattled the window behind his head. Luke grinned. "See what I mean? Ann doesn't like it already."

He turned. "I tried to tell them. . ." He trailed off.

Ann's eyes widened. She mouthed something and pointed over his shoulder with one hand while the other flapped with the speed of a hummingbird. Luke spun around. A light-colored car barreled toward them. Even though it appeared to be slowing, he shouted for Ann to get back and shoved Ross out of the way.

The car veered. Once it hit the graveled area of the parking lot, the driver turned the wheels hard enough to make the back end swing around. The car rolled down the slight incline and came to a stop with a thud against a tree.

Casey! Luke took off at a sprint. Ross and Steve's feet pounded close behind. He reached the driver's side door and jerked it open.

"Casey?"

She sat trembling, her arms limp at her sides. The deployed air bag melted like a marshmallow in her lap. She looked up at him, her eyes dazed. A scuff marred her chin and forehead, and her nose was bright red. When he offered his hand to help her out, she leaned away.

He squatted down. "Are you all right?"

"Wh–what are you doing here?" She glanced around. "Where'd you come from?"

Steve leaned an arm atop the car. "You know her, Luke?"

"Yeah. She's Lydia Alexander's niece." He stepped back to let Casey get out. "Do you always come to a stop like that? You know how fast you'll wear out your tires?" He checked the wheels. "At least you don't have a flat this time." He examined the front end of the car, still butted up against the tree. He glanced back at her with a slight grin. "At least now your bumpers match."

By the look on her face, he'd either said the wrong thing or sprouted a second head.

She turned toward her car and dragged her fingers through her hair, pushing it away from her face. "I couldn't get it to stop. I didn't have any brakes."

"What?" Luke dropped to his knees and peered under the car. Fluid dripped from the brake line, leaving a small brown puddle on the ground. The car looked new. She either bought a lemon or was accident-prone. "Looks like you snapped the brake line. Maybe you did that during your last spin."

Steve knelt beside him for a look. "Her last spin?"

"Yeah. I found her like this yesterday on the way to Lydia's."

Casey planted her fists on her slender hips. "I'm standing right here. And for your information, I don't always stop like that."

Luke stood and brushed the dirt from his hands. "Sorry. Are you sure you're okay?"

"I'm fine." She cocked her head and eyed him. The suspicious look from yesterday returned. "You never answered my question."

"What question?"

"What are you doing here?"

"Oh. I'm doing some consultant work with Ross and Steve." He turned and made the introductions. "What about you, Casey? Did you just use this drive to stop the car?"

She glanced at the two men. Her face, now colored by a touch of red, softened with his explanation. Just what was going on in that beautiful head of hers?

She traced a pattern in the gravel with the toe of her

sneaker and shoved her hands deep into her jacket pockets. "Actually, I came out here to spend some time in my and Aunt Liddy's favorite spot. I guess that won't be possible today. I've got to get this car worked on."

Luke's heart went out to her. The woman was changeable as quicksilver, but it didn't surprise him. Abandoned by her father, a mother who died two years ago, and now Lydia. No wonder she'd acted so peculiar the last couple of days. She'd been dealt some hard blows. Maybe time spent with the memory of her aunt would help bring peace. God would want him to help if he could.

He dug into the pocket of his jeans, pulled out his keys, and handed them to her. "Here, use my pickup to go into the park. I'll call Bob's Garage and have him send a tow truck. I'll ride with him to his shop, and you can meet me there when you're done."

Consternation danced in her expression. Her eyes flashed back and forth from his face to the keys lying in his palm. If he wasn't mistaken, her bottom lip trembled.

She took a hesitant step forward. "Are you sure?"

He smiled. "I'm sure." He dangled the keys in front of her face. "Let me know if there's anything else I can do."

Her eyes stayed trained on his as she accepted them. "Thank you, Luke. I—I appreciate this."

"Not a problem. Just let me get my briefcase out of the cab, and you can be on your way."

The two headed to the truck together, and by the crunching and scuffing sounds coming from behind, Steve and Ross planned to join them. It looked as though a moment of privacy was out of the question.

Minutes later, Luke watched as his tailgate disappeared around the curve heading into the park.

Lord, comfort her. She misses her aunt so much—
A shove in the back interrupted him.

Steve stood grinning at him like a bear cub with honey dripping from its face. "Luke, my boy, that's the most interest I've ever seen you have in a girl. I believe there's hope for you yet."

Ross elbowed Luke in the side, his sketch still clasped in his hand. "Yeah. Maybe she'll forget something in the truck and give you a reason to go calling on her."

He shook his head at their teasing, though an excuse to see her again didn't sound half bad. "Let me phone Bob. Then we can finish discussing your landscaping job."

The call made, Luke continued describing his thoughts of where to place the shrubs, but his mind and heart were no longer engaged in the task. A certain blond laid claim to those.

Casey scooted forward on the seat, her foot barely reaching the big Chevy's gas pedal. Luke's truck was a far cry from the BMW she had bought to reward herself after her Web design business took off. The black beast screamed macho, despite the sign on the door that read GARDEN OF EDEN NURSERY—LET US MAKE YOUR HOME PARADISE.

She frowned. Okay. So the sign was cute—just like Luke. A grin tugged at her lips. And his dimple was cute, the one in his right cheek that deepened every time he teased her. With a growl deep in her throat, she slapped the steering wheel. "Get a grip. The man's a suspect." Whether Luke realized it or not, she planned to search his truck carefully for clues.

"Steve Agee plays marbles with Ross Derkson. Steve Agee plays marbles with Ross Derkson." She repeated the phrase over and over until she was confident she wouldn't forget Steve Agee or Ross Derkson's names. Unfortunately, the Post-its were still in her car. Oh well. Brandy Purcell took great mental notes. In *Death Toll*, her photographic memory saved a young girl's life, and like Brandy, Casey would learn to observe the smallest details.

She shrugged. Her system wasn't perfect, but at least she'd remember who to ask for when she checked to see if the meeting with Luke was planned or not.

Consultant work. Humph. His presence seemed more premeditation than coincidence. Jack probably mentioned her plan to visit the park to Luke. Two accidents in two days, and he showed up at both? Only a nitwit would miss the connection.

She rolled to a stop a few yards from the path leading to the river's edge and put the truck in park. Now, where to look? She slid across the seat and popped open the glove box. Tools tumbled out, including a trowel that looked as if it had been used to dig out the Grand Canyon.

"For heaven's sake." She held the dirty trowel between her thumb and index finger. "Get a toolbox."

She dumped it on the floor with the rest of his stuff and rummaged through the proof of insurance, the owner's manual, and a receipt for a dozen roses. Roses? Why would a nursery owner go to a flower shop for roses?

The paper was crumpled and coffee stained, but she could still make out the script. "Black's Floral," she read. If she remembered right, Aunt Liddy had a standing order for cut flowers in winter—delivered every other week in a black panel van with flowers splayed across the side.

Aunt Liddy said fresh flowers were the one extravagance she couldn't live without, and when she couldn't get them from her garden, she ordered them from Black's.

She'd call when she got into town. She tossed the receipt back into the glove compartment, replaced the tools one by one, and slammed the door closed before everything spilled out again.

A pair of dirty work gloves hibernated under the seat, so stiff and dry she figured they had to have been there for months. She kept digging until her pile consisted of seed packets, a road atlas, a first aid kit, and a tire iron.

By now, sweat trickled into her eyes, and the blood pounding in her ears gave her a monstrous headache. She sat up, flipped her hair back, blew the wisps clinging to her moist forehead aside, and cracked open the windows. Nothing.

She opened the door and climbed out into the bright midmorning sun. A check of the backseat revealed the same as the front, nothing, except for a smelly work shirt and a pair of black rubber boots. Several bumps and scrapes marred the front bumper, but none of them bore telltale silver paint. He could explain them away if he chose.

"Think, Casey," she said to herself, tapping her temple. She ticked off the facts on her fingers. "One, Luke was at both accidents, but both times he offered to help afterward. Two, there's nothing suspicious in his truck, not even an unpaid parking ticket. What does that tell you?"

She snapped her fingers. It told her he didn't want her dead, just scared. Maybe too scared to investigate Aunt Liddy's death. She moved him up a notch on her mental list of suspects.

Grabbing the keys from the ignition, she shut the

door and locked it. A recent rain had muddied the trail leading to the river. Good thing she wore her sneakers.

Plymouth Rock wasn't far. Well, it wasn't really Plymouth Rock, but on her first visit at six years of age, it sure seemed like the fabled stone. Aunt Liddy had laughed at her innocent question. They called the large boulder Plymouth Rock ever since, their own little private joke. This spot in the park was their favorite place, made even more special because they had discovered it just after her father left home for good.

Sorrow welled in her chest. With Aunt Liddy gone, the rock would be just her place now, if she could bear the thought of visiting it alone after today. She crossed a narrow footbridge, climbed down the riverbank to the water, and came to a stop at the rock.

It looked a whole lot smaller than she remembered. When she was six, the rock came almost to her shoulder. Now she was twenty-seven, and it came only to her hip. She reached out with both hands and hauled herself onto the stone.

The sun heated its smooth surface. She leaned back, both palms propped behind her and feet dangling toward the waves. She loved this place. The smell of fish and water, the call of birds, the wind rustling in the grass like soft applause—it all seemed so peaceful.

"Just how you liked it," she whispered into the breeze. Tears pricked her eyes. She tipped her head back to stare at the cloudless sky. Did God love her enough to help her find out what happened to Aunt Liddy? Did He even care?

A frog croaked and jumped into the river with a small splash. She wiped the tears from her eyes and leaned forward to watch. He scrambled onto a fallen log several yards away, hesitated a moment, then leaped again, out of sight. But Casey's gaze stayed fixed to a spot at the bottom of the log.

She bolted upright. Her hands clenched into fists. Fear tightened in her chest until she couldn't breathe. What was that? She slid to the ground, her knees so shaky they almost didn't hold her. Unwilling to take a step forward, she rose up on her toes and craned her neck. It looked like. . .could it be? Obscured by grass and protruding from under the log was an object that looked a lot like Aunt Liddy's shoe.

Her mouth devoid of moisture, Casey wondered what lay on the other side of the log. Worse, she knew she'd have to find out.

5

Luke backed out of the Hilltop Café, still swabbing at the Coke stain on his pants with a napkin. He'd made one little remark, and his dad's secretary had come unwound like a top with the string jerked off. The woman was entirely too jittery.

"Thanks for buying lunch, Carol. Hope your day gets better." He glanced down at his legs. "Tell Dad not to work you so hard."

Shifting a banker's box stuffed with files to her hip, Carol tugged her purse strap over her shoulder and shrugged. "Sorry about the spill. I guess I need to learn to talk without my hands."

"No problem." He pointed to the box. "Sure I can't help with those? I don't mind walking you to your car."

Carol cast a nervous glance down both sides of the street. "I've got it. Thanks for offering—"

At that moment, her oversized purse dropped from her shoulder onto her forearm, knocking the precariously balanced box askew.

"Whoa." Luke made a grab for the files. To his surprise, Carol let go and clutched her purse with both hands.

"Don't!"

"No, I—"

"I don't need—"

The scramble for the purse, box, and manila folders might have been funny if Carol hadn't dumped everything in her arms to the sidewalk. She yelped and dropped to her knees. Lipsticks, powder compacts, and a myriad of other female necessities rolled onto the pavement, coming to a stop next to a fat envelope stuffed with bills.

Brows raised, Luke picked it up and handed it to her. "That's a lot of dough to be carrying around in your purse."

"It's the deposit. I haven't made it to the bank yet." Carol grabbed the envelope and shoved it into the purse. "Matter of fact, I need to do that now." She rose, the box and its contents back in her arms, a little less neatly than before. "You'll remember what I said? Let me know if you notice a change in your dad's mood, his routine, whatever. He's gotta be hurting, what with Lydia's death and all. My friend is a good counselor. She could help."

"I'll let you know."

The two exchanged a wave. Luke headed back to Bob's Garage determined never to mention his dad, Lydia, or Casey in Carol's presence again. Those topics upset her, which had led to her drink ending up in his lap.

Down the street, an engine roared and tires squealed. Luke glanced over his shoulder.

"Hey!" He spun around. "That's my truck!"

Puffs of black churned from the tires as the truck screeched to a halt in front of the police station.

Good grief. Doesn't the woman know how to drive at a normal speed?

Casey swung out of the cab and raced toward the building, leaving the door to his pickup wide open. Stunned, Luke stood still a moment before running after her. He paused to give the door a quick shove, but then he noticed the keys still dangling in the ignition. He grabbed them, shut the door, and resumed his chase.

Casey's voice slammed into his ears the moment he entered the station.

"Of course I'm sure it's Aunt Liddy's shoe. I bought

them for her last year."

Rafferty rumbled a reply, but Luke couldn't make out the words. Casey must not have liked what he said.

"That doesn't matter. So what if she might've forgotten them? You have to go to the river and check it out. What if she's still out there somewhere?"

Oh no, Lord, please.

The thought turned his stomach. He arrived at Rafferty's door in time to see Casey wipe tears from her eyes.

She reached to finger the dark leather shoe. "What if someone hid her body out there?"

The last question, much more subdued than earlier, thumped head-on into Luke's chest. He swallowed hard at the sight of Lydia's muddy shoe sitting on Rafferty's desk. The full impact of her death hit him all over again. She really was gone. He pulled his cap off, folded it in half, and jammed it into his back pocket. Was Casey right? Was Lydia's death the result of murder instead of suicide?

In the sudden quiet, he realized that both Casey and Rafferty were staring at him. Well, not at him, exactly, but his pants. He looked down and then back up. "Oh, uh, slight mishap at lunch."

He moved next to the desk to get a better look at the shoe. Casey backed away, her hand stretched toward Rafferty. And there was that look of fear and accusation in her eyes again. *What in blue blazes is her problem?*

Then a thought struck him. Surely she didn't think. . . She couldn't possibly believe. . .

"Detective, I think you'd better find out where Luke Kerrigan was the night my aunt disappeared."

Both Luke and Detective Rafferty gawked at her, mouths agape, but Casey didn't care. She put on her best Brandy Purcell face and lifted her chin.

Luke's eyebrows shot up. "You can't think I had anything to do with Lydia's death. She was like a mother to—"

"Don't say it. Don't even say it." She put up her hand and whirled to face Rafferty. "If you won't drag the river, then you at least have to ask some questions."

A look of utter exasperation crossed Rafferty's face. He blew out a sigh. "Okay. Luke, where were you?"

"When?"

"The night Lydia disappeared."

"I was with you."

"What?" Casey's satisfied smirk disappeared. She pointed to Luke, then Rafferty. "You two—"

"Were at a church barbecue celebrating the opening of their new Family Life Center," Rafferty said.

Her hopes fell further by the minute. She stared at Luke. "All day?"

"I did the landscaping." He pulled the cap from his pocket and pointed at the logo. "Garden of Eden Nursery," he said with a shrug and a sheepish grin.

"But. . .then you couldn't. . ."

Luke replaced the cap and shoved his hands into his pockets. "I couldn't. I wouldn't." He looked her in the eye. "I didn't."

Rafferty put both palms on top of the desk and pushed himself up. "No one did, Miss Alexander. That's what I've been trying to tell you."

Casey stumbled back. "What about the truck?"

"What truck?" Rafferty said.

"The one that tried to run me off the road yesterday." She tossed a look at Luke. "His."

"What!" the men said in unison.

Luke jerked his thumb to his chest. "My truck?"

"Oh yeah, that's right." She crossed her arms. "You were digging up flowers when someone tried to splatter me all over the side of the mountain. Like *that's* believable."

Luke shook his head. "I *was* digging up flowers. I mean shrubs. Oh, for heaven's sake. You mean that's why you wrote 'black Chevy' on the Post-it?"

"All right, all right." Rafferty halted their tirade with a wave. "Miss Alexander, when exactly did this take place?"

"I told you, yesterday afternoon."

"Late?"

"Around 4:30. Why?"

Rafferty walked to the dented filing cabinet. It opened with a squeal. He pulled a photo out of the drawer. "The truck you saw, is this it?"

She grabbed the photo, studied it, and nodded. "That's the one all right." She gave the picture back, planted both hands on her hips, and tipped her head to stare at Luke. "I take very good mental notes."

"Well, that's good," said Rafferty, "except it's not Luke's truck."

"What?"

Luke moved to the desk. "Let me see the picture."

Rafferty handed it to him. "That's Maxwell Novak's truck. He owns the hair salon where Lydia used to work. He stopped by here yesterday around four to fill out a police report. Said his truck was stolen."

"So you think somebody stole Mr. Novak's truck and used it to run me off the road?"

"Not necessarily. I doubt the thief was trying to kill you. Most likely he was trying to hightail it out of town, and you got in his way."

"But why?" Luke rounded the desk. "Have you asked around? Did anybody see anything?"

Rafferty grabbed the picture from Luke's hand and jabbed a beefy finger toward his nose. "Don't you start. Bad enough I've got her telling me how to do my job."

Casey gulped. She was "her." Didn't matter. She pressed on. "That doesn't explain my broken brake line. I had another accident today."

"Excuse me?" Rafferty gave a bewildered scowl, his gaze swiveling between Luke and Casey. "Did I miss something?"

"Her brake line was leaking. She ran into a tree at the state park."

Rafferty dropped the photo on the desk. "Were you hurt?"

Casey rubbed her sore chin. "The air bag deployed, but no, I wasn't hurt."

"Where is your car now?"

"At Bob's Garage."

"I'll check into it and get back to you."

Luke grabbed her elbow and pulled her toward the door. "Okay. Thanks, Detective. We'll just leave you to it, then."

"What about the river?" Casey resisted long enough to ask.

"I'll have the rangers keep an eye on the banks." Rafferty threw his hand up when she opened her mouth to protest. "That's all, Miss Alexander."

A moment later, she and Luke stood on the sidewalk

next to his truck. Casey gestured toward the closed doors.
"I—"

Luke held up the keys. They jangled from his fingers.

"Oh." Her gaze dropped to her muddy shoes. "Well,
guess I'd better check on my car. Thanks for letting me use
your truck." Too embarrassed to look at him, she swung
around and headed down the street.

"Ahem."

She looked back. Luke leaned against the hood, both
arms crossed over his chest. The cool breeze tousled his
brown hair, causing it to fall over his forehead. He cocked
an eyebrow. Did he want her to apologize? She figured she
owed him that. She trudged back to where he stood.

"Luke—"

"Do you trust me enough to let me give you a ride?"

She raised her head. To her amazement, he was
smiling, and the dimple she found so attractive appeared.
"Huh?"

"To the garage."

"Oh." She nodded.

He straightened, took his time rounding to the passenger side, and swung the door wide.

Casey sighed. Oh, all right. Did he have to make
such a show of it? She climbed in, ignoring the hand he
offered.

Neither spoke as the truck hummed over the blacktop.
Finally, she could stand the silence no longer. "I'm sorry,
Luke."

He glanced sideways at her. "Don't apologize."

"Why not?" She turned in the seat to look at him.

They rolled to a stop at the town's one red light. Luke
gripped the wheel with both hands. "Because I believe you.

I no longer think Lydia committed suicide. And I think whoever killed her is trying to keep you from finding out what really happened."

She clenched her fists in her lap. He believed her! Of all people, the one she'd mistrusted the most, the one she'd been most wrong about, believed her. "You do?" Relief thickened her voice.

He nodded. "I wish you'd told me about the truck yesterday."

He gazed at her, his eyes so deep and full of emotion, it hurt to look at them.

She leaned forward and peeked under the visor to stare at the light. "Green."

To her relief, Luke turned his attention to the road. Within minutes, they pulled up to the garage.

Bob, the ancient owner of the tiny repair shop, wandered out, wiping his hands on a filthy rag. Grease dirtied his nails, and he reeked of gasoline and oil. Luke quickly dispensed with the introductions.

"Ma'am." He inclined his head toward Casey, who smiled back. "Got that brake line fixed."

"You did?" Casey hardly dared believe her luck. Who'd have thought a place like this could work on imports?

"Your airbag's another story."

Her stomach plummeted. "My air bag?"

She followed Bob out of the parking lot into the garage, Luke close behind. Her car, her precious reward to herself, looked pathetic straddling a cement pit in the floor. Both bumpers were crumpled, and her steering wheel gaped at her, a vacant hole in the middle like a grinning first-grader without any teeth.

"I saved your emblem though." Bob fished the symbol

out of the front pocket of his overalls. "I found it in the seat, along with these." He clasped a fistful of yellow Post-its in one meaty hand.

Luke guffawed, but when Casey cast him a withering glance, he promptly wiped the smile from his face. She took the emblem and notes from Bob and put them in her purse. "So how long before you can get the air bag fixed?"

"That depends on how long it takes for the parts shop in Worcester to get the thing ordered. After that, shouldn't be long 'tall."

A throbbing started in Casey's head. "Is it drivable?"

Bob's bushy eyebrows rose. "I wouldn't recommend it."

"Neither would I," Luke said, piping in for the first time. "Your insurance will cover the cost of a rental car. You do have insurance, right?"

"Of course," Casey snapped. Honestly. Just because she'd accused him of murder didn't mean she was an idiot.

"Okay, then. Bob, order the part. Casey, come with me."

"Where are we going?"

"To find you something to drive. Thanks, Bob."

Bob aimed a tobacco-stained grin at them. Luke and Casey got back in his truck, and less than an hour later, Casey clutched the keys to a small, dark blue Honda.

"You sure you're okay?"

Her cheeks warmed at the concern in his voice. She glanced up at him. "Yeah. I'll be fine."

Luke motioned toward town. "You wanna get something to eat?"

She shook her head despite the rumbling in her

stomach. "I just want to get this day over with. Thanks anyway."

He nodded and held the door while she climbed into the car. "Casey?"

"Yeah?"

"Drive safe."

His smile was infectious. She grinned back. "I will."

"I'll stop by first thing in the morning."

She paused with her hand at the ignition. "Why?"

He leaned in, close enough for her to breathe in the warm, spicy scent of him. "You don't think I'm gonna let you go after a killer alone, do you? Besides, the tree Lydia ordered before she died is ready. I thought I'd go ahead and plant it. She would have wanted that."

He looked so serious all of sudden, so protective. It sent shivers down her back. "Right. Okay. I'll see you in the morning."

He closed the door. Good thing. Any longer and she'd have been drooling. She shook the memory of his tantalizing aftershave from her thoughts and turned the rental toward home.

Hurried by the ringing of the telephone, Casey jammed her key into the front door of Aunt Liddy's house and stumbled inside. "Coming," she panted as she dropped her things in the hall and grabbed for the handset. "Hello?"

"Casey? It's Monah Trenary."

"Monah?"

"From the bank."

"Oh, Monah! Hello. How are you?"

"Good, thanks. You didn't call. I just wanted to make sure you're all right."

Casey thought over the events of the past two days. "I'm fine. Just been a little run-down lately."

Monah hesitated, as though unsure what to make of the odd remark. "Uh. . .well, we talked about getting together to discuss the people Lydia knew. Do you still want to do that?"

"Absolutely."

"How does tomorrow morning sound? I can stop by before I go to work."

Casey wrapped the coiled phone cord around her finger. "Not sure about that. A friend of Aunt Liddy's, Luke Kerrigan, promised to come by to plant a tree she ordered."

"Luke? He and I are old friends. We went to school together. He won't mind."

"Really. You know Luke? I'm starting to think everybody knows everybody."

Monah laughed. "Small town, you know."

"Oh, I'm starting to." She pressed her back to the table. "So you'll come by tomorrow?"

"Bright and early."

"Sounds great, Monah." Casey rang off, cheered to know that she'd made at least one friend in Pine Mills.

A hot shower and the tea she fixed for herself afterward did wonders for her headache. She breathed in the soothing scent of chamomile and tipped her toweled head against the couch with a sigh. What a day.

Over the fireplace, Aunt Liddy's mantel clock chimed softly. She cracked an eyelid. Ten o'clock. Time for bed.

She rinsed her cup in the sink, padded to the bedroom,

and pulled her cotton pj's out of the dresser. Stifling yawn after yawn, Casey exchanged her terry bathrobe and towel for the pajamas, peeled back the covers, and climbed into bed.

After two tries, the lamp switch turned between her fingers and she dropped onto her cool pillowcase. Sleep tugged at her senses, but flashes from the day played across her mind. Luke. Aunt Liddy's shoe. Detective Rafferty's face when she told him where she found it. Luke. Luke.

She snuggled deeper under the down comforter. Boy, was she glad to be wrong about him. Or was she? What if all that stuff at the police station was just an act to throw her off? She pushed the unwanted thought away. He said he'd stop by in the morning. She'd have to remember to have coffee ready. Maybe then she could tell him all about what happened at the park.

The shoe.

Her eyes fluttered open. Shadows caused by the swaying of the oak tree outside her window danced across the ceiling. She stared at them. Something bothered her. Something she couldn't put her finger on. The more she thought about it, the less sleepy she became. She rolled onto her side.

Light from the silver moon shone across the floor, illuminating the rich colors of the Oriental rug. Tears pricked her eyes. She was alone in this big house. Aunt Liddy wasn't asleep in the room down the hall. She shuddered as she remembered the horror she'd felt when she first spotted the shoe.

And then the strange elation when she'd tramped frantically through the grass, relieved not to find a body. But she hadn't checked the ground surrounding the shoe.

What if the shoe wasn't the only thing hidden next to the log?

Nah. I would have noticed it right then. She wrestled with her pillow and flopped onto her other side.

She'd been in a hurry to tell Rafferty what she'd found, she argued. Could she have missed something? She bolted upright. When she picked up the shoe, mud slid out. Mud and. . .something. She flipped on the light.

Her watch on the nightstand said almost 10:30. Could she wait until morning? What if the tide came in and carried off whatever was in the shoe? Did the tides affect the water level this far inland? Maybe not, but what about an animal? She shivered. She couldn't take the chance.

She flung off the covers, wincing as the cool night air hit her bare legs, and hurried back into her clothes. Her sneakers, still damp from the cleaning she gave them when she got home, would have to do. She tugged them on and rushed out the door, pausing just long enough to grab a flashlight from the closet under the stairs.

Half an hour later, she rolled to a stop about a hundred feet from the state park. The sound of gravel crunching under the tires echoed loudly in the cool night air. At least no one was around to hear it except for a few noisy crickets. She parked far from the road so that anyone driving by would miss the small compact huddled beneath the shadow of a stand of maples.

One fat owl watched her progress from the park's stone entrance. "Hoo?"

"Me. Now hush."

She scurried over the low gate that stretched across the driveway. Nothing more than two V-shaped tubes padlocked together at the center, the gate was meant to keep out cars and not much else. Once she was well clear of the road, she flicked on her flashlight and wound her way to the river.

The damp air brought a chill to Casey's flesh. She rubbed her arms and quickened her steps. Wet leaves and river grass scented the air, and all around a chorus of bullfrogs croaked in disjointed harmony.

The log lay right where she remembered it. She dropped to her knees in the dank earth and dug through the mud, shining the light back and forth until she spotted it—a glimpse of white amid all the dirt.

Her hands shook as she grasped the object and brought it near for closer inspection. It was one of Aunt Liddy's lace handkerchiefs, and there was something inside. She clutched the flashlight between her teeth and carefully unfolded the cloth. In her palm lay a rock.

What in the world? Why would Aunt Liddy hide a rock in her shoe? She wrapped the stone back into its protective cover. Best to get out of here and figure it out at home.

Snap!

She jumped and shined the light into the trees. Nothing, if she didn't count the spooky shadows. Her flesh tingled. Someone was watching her. She straightened.

"Hello?"

The frogs' croaking grew louder.

"Hello?" She repeated. "Anybody out there?" She took a step back, toward her car.

Crack!

The second noise sent her rushing from the river, her wet shoes rubbing blisters on her heels.

Heart pounding, she threw a glance over her shoulder at the empty trail. She slowed, came to a stop, breathing heavily. Nobody chased her. It was her imagination. She gave a shaky laugh. At least she hadn't fallen down. She hated when that happened in the movies.

The blow came so quickly, she never saw it coming. From the opposite end of the trail, someone tackled her. She sprawled in the dirt. The flashlight skittered in one direction, the stone and handkerchief in the other. She screamed and curled her fingers to claw her attacker's face but grabbed only a thick ski mask.

The attacker shoved her aside and crawled over her. Casey scrambled away. The person didn't seem the least bit interested in her. Instead, he seemed to want. . .

She saw it in the glow of the flashlight a split second before it disappeared inside the assailant's fist. The stone.

The flashlight lay at a crazy angle, sending a fragmented beam across the attacker's shoes. She stared, her eyes round as the menacing figure started toward her. And then. . .

The figure froze, staring at a point above her head. Casey whirled to look. Behind her, a shadow dislodged from the trees and plunged into the woods. When she turned back around, her attacker was gone.

6

Luke bounded up the porch steps, two covered coffee cups balanced in one hand and a sack of chocolate doughnuts clasped in the other. The sugary scent wafted from the bag as he used the toe of his work boot to bang on the door. "Voice of Truth," the last tune he heard on the radio, played through his head, and he couldn't help but whistle along. The song died after several moments when Casey still didn't answer.

He shoved their breakfast under his arm and rapped on the door again. "Casey?" He moved to the window and peered inside.

There she sat, propped up on the couch with several pillows and a blanket draped from neck to toe, head back and mouth open. Several taps on the window brought no reaction. A spark triggered in his mind and zipped down his spine. This whole scene seemed odd.

He knew right where to find the spare key. He'd helped Lydia hide it. He set the coffee and doughnuts on the swing and pulled the extra piece of wood out from under the new flower box. Nestled in the perfectly etched-out groove lay the key. He unlocked the door and went inside to kneel beside Casey. The blanket rose and fell in time with her breathing. At least she was alive. He gave her shoulder a shake.

"Casey."

She didn't move.

He shook her again. "Time to wake up."

Eyes suddenly wide open, she bolted from the couch, arms swinging. The blanket fell, entangling her feet. Luke caught her before she hit the floor and snared a fist on his cheekbone for his trouble.

"Whoa." Luke pinned her arms to her sides. "Casey, it's me, Luke."

Chest heaving, she turned and gave him a good look. She blinked several times.

"Luke."

"Yes." He couldn't help but smile. She looked adorable nestled in his arms, even with mud smeared on her face and leaves and dead grass tangled in her hair.

She squirmed. "Let me up."

He complied and stood with her.

"How'd you get in here? I know I locked that door."

Luke held up the spare key. "I built the flower boxes where Lydia hid it." He handed it to her. "I knocked, but you didn't answer."

She stared at the key lying in the palm of her hand then glanced around, her gaze darting from the door to the windows.

He eyed her from head to toe. "I guess you were too tired to clean up before you went to sleep last night."

A piece of grass fell from her hair and drifted to the floor. He pulled a leaf from a spot just above her ear and held it out to show her. Her gaze bored into his, and he thought he read a question in her eyes. She must have found the answer, because she relaxed and dropped onto the couch.

"I was attacked last night."

The simple statement slammed into his chest and left him without air. "What? Attacked? When? Where?"

A tremulous smile touched her lips. "One question at a time, please."

He took a deep breath and sat next to her. "Tell me what happened."

She spilled the story, the key twisting and turning in her fingers while she spoke. The fear he heard in her voice sparked alarm and irritation. By the time she told him about her attacker disappearing, all he wanted to do was pull her into his arms and protect her with everything in him. He settled for squeezing her hand. "Thank God you're safe. He was watching over you, you know. You never should have gone out there alone."

A flush stole over her face. She dipped her head and leaned forward as she finished her story. "So anyway, I came home, locked the doors, and slept on the couch. And now," she said, touching her mud-caked hair as she stood, "I'm going to clean up."

"Oh." Luke rose to his feet. "Okay. Would you mind if I talked to Rafferty? He should know about this."

Casey stopped him with a tap on his arm. "I'd really like to hold off on that for now. But can you stick around until I finish? I just—"

A raging bull couldn't have chased him away.

"I'll be waiting in the kitchen with hot coffee and doughnuts."

She frowned. "I don't have any doughnuts."

He smiled and winked. "You do now." The two exchanged a look that sent warmth all the way to the bottom of his empty stomach. "Go on. I'll be here."

She headed toward the stairs. A shriveled leaf stuck to the bottom of her heel fluttered with each step she took. He stifled a smile.

Luke went to the porch in search of the promised doughnuts. A red Corvette pulled into the driveway. His father. Just what he needed—another chance for his dad to add more pressure to sell his nursery business, driving an even bigger wedge between them. As if they were ever that close. He waited for his dad to join him before leading the way to the kitchen.

"What brings you out here, Dad?"

"Probably the same thing as you. I ran into Mike Brockman. He told me about Casey being run off the road and finding Lydia's shoe near the river. You know about that?"

Luke poured water into the pot to make coffee. The two cups he picked up from the doughnut shop weren't going to be enough. "Yeah. I changed her tire for her and saw her go into the police station yesterday about the shoe."

"She okay?"

"A little shook up." After measuring the grounds and turning on the coffeemaker, Luke sat at the table with his dad and related the same story Casey had told him. She came down the stairs just as he finished, transformed from a drooping flower to one in full bloom. He poured her a cup of coffee and placed it on the table alongside the doughnuts.

Casey smiled her thanks before turning her attention to his father. "Hey, Jack. This is a surprise."

He stood and gave her a hug. "I hear you've had plenty of excitement since showing up in town."

She gave a disgusted grunt. "If you want to call it that. Did Luke fill you in?"

"Sure did. Why would someone want a rock bad enough to attack you?"

She shrugged and took a sip. "I guess they didn't know

it was just a rock."

His dad looked puzzled. "Describe it to me."

Casey frowned. "I only saw it by flashlight, so I didn't get a good look." She leaned back and stared into space. "It was kinda oblong. . .and pitted. It almost looked black, but also a little shiny." She reached for a doughnut, pinched off a piece, and popped it in her mouth. "Maybe it was just something she liked to carry with her, like a worry rock."

Luke eyed his dad. A small crease marred his forehead, but he couldn't tell if it came from concern or deliberation. "How about it? Did Lydia have something like that?"

"I don't know for sure. She loved to pick up pretty rocks and shells along the beach. She may have found it recently."

Luke reached into his pocket and pulled out his cell phone. "Either way, we still need to report this to Rafferty." He punched in the number and handed it to Casey. "Just push the CALL button."

His dad leaned across the table and held up his hand. "Hold on a minute. Let's think this through."

"What's there to think about? Casey was attacked. The police need to know."

"Wait, Luke. I want to hear what your dad has to say." She set the phone down. "What's on your mind, Jack?"

He propped both elbows on the table. With his thumb, he traced the edge of his jaw. "You were in the park illegally, Casey. That may not go over very well."

Luke thumped the table. "She was attacked."

"And came away unhurt." He turned back to Casey. "All I'm saying is, think about it. Do you really want to go through the hassle of reporting this only to have them slap a fine or worse on you, all over a stolen rock?" He stood. "I've got to go. I'm already late. Just give it some thought before you make the call. You've been up against Rafferty twice now. I can't imagine a third experience will be much fun."

"No, it wouldn't."

He pushed the chair in. "Good. That's settled. One last thing. . ." He cleared his throat and turned away from Luke. "Have you thought about that offer I made?"

Her brow crinkled and cleared a second later. "Oh. About buying the house."

"Yes. Can we draw up some papers?"

"Wait a minute." Luke sat up in alarm. "You're selling the house?"

She shook her head. "I haven't decided yet. I'm sorry, Jack. I really don't want to think about that right now."

He hesitated, drumming his fingers on the table, then gave in with a sigh. "All right. Just let me know."

Luke fumed while his dad kissed the top of Casey's head, said his good-byes, and left. He didn't get a chance to speak his mind before Monah appeared and tapped on the kitchen doorway.

"Hey." She entered, dropped her canvas shoulder bag on the floor, and took the vacated chair. "Jack let me in." Her gaze bounced between him and Casey. "Um, bad time? Should I come back later?"

"No." Casey touched her arm. "Don't go. I was just thinking."

Luke stood, grabbed another cup, filled it with steaming coffee, and slid it across the table to Monah. "She was attacked last night, and Dad tried to talk her out of reporting it."

"Attacked?"

Casey rolled her eyes. "Thanks, Luke. At this rate, the

news will get to Rafferty all on its own."

She gave a brief version of the story to Monah and added the dilemma of whether or not to report it.

Monah swallowed a mouthful of doughnut. "Who do you think it was? Did you get a good look at either of them?"

"No." Casey glanced at Luke. "It could have been him for all I know."

"Me?"

"Luke?" Monah snorted. "No way."

Luke shook his head. "She's already accused me of killing Lydia."

Monah choked on another bite. "Luke?" Her voice came out in a squeak. "You've got to be kidding." She swallowed and washed the doughnut down with a gulp of coffee. "Actually, I thought it might be Max."

"Who?"

"Maxwell Novak. The guy Lydia used to work for. She left on pretty bad terms."

"She never mentioned it. Tell me what happened."

"Well, you know how I told you that Lydia became a believer. She was on fire and wanted to tell everyone about it. Max hated it, said she was harassing the customers, and told her to stop talking about it. That's when Lydia decided to start her own business here at the house. She took a good many of Max's customers with her. Made him so mad. He was overheard threatening to find a way to shut her down." Monah picked up what was left of a doughnut. "Maybe he found a way." She took a bite and licked the chocolate off her finger. "What happened to your cheek, Luke?"

Luke always had a hard time keeping up with Monah. Not only did she talk fast, but she changed topics faster than Casey came to stops. He touched his cheek and glanced at Casey.

Monah hooted. "Casey did that? You two not getting along?" She picked up a napkin and swatted him on the arm.

Luke bit back a grin and leaned forward. "Just why are you here, Monah?"

"Casey and I are going over all the people Lydia knew, which reminds me"—she covered a cough with a napkin—"Pastor Burgess called. He said the members of the church would like to have an informal memorial service for Lydia. The ladies have volunteered to provide finger foods and beverages, if you're willing, that is."

Casey's eyes filled. "When?"

"Saturday. I know that's not much time to prepare, but everyone's offering to help. They only ask that you look for some pictures they can place around the new Family Life Center. I have a great one we can use."

Luke tapped the table. He waited for Casey's response with interest, since Lydia had told him that Casey had stopped going to church. She seemed to struggle with the idea. But when she nodded, a smile spread across his face. Lydia would have been pleased.

Monah brushed at the fur clinging to his arm. "What are you grinning at, you cat? You sprouting hairs, or did you get a new feline?"

"No." Luke picked at the hairs sticking to his jacket. "Mrs. Teaser's cats have been using my nursery as a litter box." He looked at Casey. "She's had a houseful of them ever since her husband died. She used to be known as the cleaning lady. Even used to clean my dad's house. Now everyone calls her the cat lady."

"With good reason," Monah added. "You know, the last time I called on her, one of those cats sat in the doorway heaving until it hacked up a thimble. *A thimble*. Can you believe it? I haven't been able to go back since."

Luke grinned at Monah's shudder. "That would be Lionel. He's notorious for swallowing stuff, only to throw it up later."

He nodded at Casey's "Eww" and Monah's "Gross." "I know. Now every morning I have to do a search and destroy on their messes so my customers won't find it on their shoes." He smirked at the look on the girls' faces. "Exactly. Mrs. Teaser saw me this morning and called me over. Said one of her cats died and would I be a dear and take care of it for her."

Casey smiled, and Monah laughed outright. Luke shook his head at them.

"Then she said her kitchen faucet had a drip and asked me to fix it for her."

Monah peered over her black-rimmed glasses at him. "And?"

Luke ran his thumbnail along the grain of wood on the tabletop, unable to look either of the girls in the eyes. "I told her I'd do it as soon as I could find the time."

Monah howled. "Only you, Luke. You're the only one I know who would put up with all of that. Why don't you build a wall or something?"

"I thought about it"—he still couldn't look up at them—"but I didn't want to hurt her feelings."

Monah bumped Casey's arm. "How could you possibly suspect a softy like Luke of killing someone? He can't even bear to hurt someone's feelings."

The look he and Casey shared sent a shaft of heat

right into his heart. He smiled as he stood. "I've got a tree to plant, and you," he said, reaching over to Monah and pushing her glasses back up on her nose, "behave."

He picked up his cell phone from the table and held it out to Casey. "What about calling Rafferty?"

"Let me think on it a little more."

He stared at her until she looked away, then flipped the phone closed and shoved it in his pocket. "All right. But I doubt much would be said about your trip to the park. I think most anyone in your position would do the same."

She only nodded.

"Okay, holler if you need anything. I'll be right outside."

Luke strode out the door, wishing that just once he and Casey could spend some time alone.

Luke's broad shoulders disappeared out the kitchen door into Aunt Liddy's garden. Casey shook her head. The man had some nerve bringing her doughnuts when he looked. . .like that. Did his good looks affect Monah the same way? They sure seemed close, judging by the scene she'd just witnessed. She peeked over at her. Monah's eyes were glued to the last glazed doughnut.

"You gonna eat that?"

Laughing, Casey grabbed the coffeepot. She needn't have worried. She refreshed Monah's cup and then her own. "Help yourself. How do you do it?" She watched as Monah devoured the treat and then licked the sugar from her fingers.

"Do what?"

"I gained ten pounds just watching you."

Monah laughed and patted her belly. "Good genes. And speaking of jeans. . ." She grinned and tipped her head toward the garden. "Eh?"

Butterflies didn't begin to describe the tremor in Casey's stomach. She played nonchalant. "He's all right." The carafe clunked as she slid it back onto the warming pad. "So, you and him?"

"Who and him? Me?" She made a face. "No! He's like my brother. I was talking about you."

Casey flushed. "I'm too busy to think about that right now. Tell me about Maxwell Novak. You really think he was angry enough about losing a few customers to hurt Aunt Liddy?"

"Not a few, a lot. And business was already slow, thanks to all the new hair salons popping up in the neighboring towns. People just don't bother making the trip when they can do everything at the mall. Maxwell griped all the time that Lydia was costing him the few regulars who still preferred the local touch."

"Hmm." Casey opened her mental list of suspects and added Maxwell Novak's name. "Maybe I should pay a visit to Aunt Liddy's old boss. Thanks, Monah."

"Sure. Hey, what was Jack doing here?" Monah scooped a heaping spoonful of sugar out of the bowl and dumped it into her cup. She swirled the spoon through her coffee and took a swallow.

"Checking on me. He heard about my accident and stopped by to make sure I was okay."

"Accident? You mean other than the incident last night?"

Monah didn't know of the events of the past two days. Casey quickly filled her in.

Monah flicked her long dark hair over her shoulder and set her cup down with a thump. No smile danced in the eyes behind the black-rimmed glasses now. "That's serious stuff, Casey. I'm going to start a prayer vigil over you."

Casey gave an uneasy laugh. She believed in prayer, but she doubted it would protect her from masked attackers. "Um, okay. Thanks." She went to the sink and dug through the cupboard for soap to wash out her mug. Through the window, she caught a glimpse of Luke, his back to her, foot braced against a shovel to push it deep into the soil.

Monah buzzed along, chatty as ever. "I figured maybe he saw Luke's car and stopped by to talk to him."

"Oh? Why?"

The small tree leaning on the ground next to him would look beautiful in the garden. Casey smiled in approval. Aunt Liddy had picked out the perfect spot. She turned on the tap and let it run until warm water flowed over her fingers.

"Well, they haven't always seen things the same way, especially when it came to the nursery. Now that Luke isn't getting the loan he wanted, Jack is really pushing for him to join in the family business."

Her attention piqued, Casey turned off the water. "What loan?"

Monah carried her now-empty cup to the counter. "The one Luke wanted to expand his nursery. I overheard him talking to the loan officer at the bank." She shrugged and set her cup in the sink. "For some reason, Luke wouldn't let his dad cosign, and the bank turned down the loan, figuring it was too big a risk with just the nursery itself as collateral. The loan officer told him they'd be glad to give it to him if he'd come back with his dad, but Luke refused." She gave Casey a quick hug and turned to go. "I'll call you with the details on the memorial service. We were thinking something informal, just friends and family. Have you got any special music or scripture passages you'd like to include?"

Casey wiped her hands on a towel. "Let me think on that, will you? I'll call you this afternoon."

Monah nodded, grabbed her bag, and headed for the front door. "Talk to you soon."

Casey let her out and returned to the kitchen. So Luke was having money problems? Her eyes went to the window.

What in the world?

She leaned forward and gripped the edge of the sink.

A burlap-wrapped object lay on the ground at Luke's feet. He picked it up and dropped it into the hole, placed the tree on top of it, and shoveled several loads of dirt in after.

Since when did fertilizer come in a burlap bag? And if it wasn't fertilizer. . .

Eww! She grimaced and tore her gaze away. Surely he didn't intend to bury the cat in the garden?

7

Rain.

Casey sighed and let the curtain fall back into place. Damp and dismal weather to match her mood. Normally she enjoyed the clean scent after a spring shower. Not today.

At least the water would be good for the birch Luke had planted. When she saw him at the church, she'd thank him for taking care of one of Aunt Liddy's final wishes.

She grabbed a tissue and dabbed at the tears pooling in her eyes. She'd moped all morning, depressed by the gloom, the musty smell of the big old house, a memorial service she could not avoid.

She didn't want to do this.

The realization hit her like the golf club used as the weapon in Brandy Purcell's book *Murder to a Tee*. It meant accepting Aunt Liddy's death and moving forward. All she wanted was to go back—back to the days when she could always count on Aunt Liddy's being there.

She closed her eyes and leaned her head against the window, the glass cool even through the cotton sheers. Warmed by her breath, the pane fogged. Aunt Liddy never minded when she blew on the windows and traced patterns through the moisture. If she tried hard enough, she might even be able to imagine Aunt Liddy standing there with her.

The mantel clock chimed the half hour. Heaving a resigned breath, she slid into her raincoat. Time to get to the church. She snatched her keys and handbag off the hall table and headed for the rental car.

A host of well-wishers met her at the entrance of Community Fellowship. Doris, a friend of Aunt Liddy's whom Casey remembered from her many visits, walked with her through the maze of hallways to the Family Life Center.

"I'm glad you decided to go ahead with this, honey. Lydia was a sweet woman. She deserves to have her memory honored." The scent of Wind Song wafted from her as she patted Casey's hand and tucked it into the crook of her arm.

Casey nodded. They passed the offices, library, and children's church with a brightly painted Noah's ark on the door. Outside the Family Life Center hung a large bulletin board, where photos of new members were posted. Lydia's smiling face stared at her from the display.

Grief burned Casey's throat. *No words. Find Monah.*

She scanned the large room. From front to back, people crowded the place. Casey swallowed, surprised at how tight her chest felt upon seeing so many of Aunt Liddy's friends gathered.

Flowers graced the windows and doorways of the Family Life Center. Soft music played in the background. Near the entrance, someone had placed a table with a book for visitors to sign. Next to it stood a picture of Aunt Liddy. She wore a big smile and held up a puffy cloud of cotton candy for the photographer. Behind her, people, cornstalks, and bright orange pumpkins painted the backdrop. Casey smiled at the fun picture. That was how she wanted Aunt Liddy remembered.

Doris led her to the front and promised to return after she finished in the kitchen. Casey nodded and let her go.

A line of people walked past, words of condolence on their lips. Many looked familiar. Some did not. She breathed a sigh of relief when Monah appeared. Dressed in straight-leg trousers and a black turtleneck, with silver hoop earrings dangling from her ears, she looked as though she'd stepped from the pages of a fashion magazine. At her side walked Pastor Burgess.

He was a big man, taller than Casey expected the first time she had met him. He'd stopped by the house shortly after she arrived in town to see if she needed anything. From their phone conversations, she'd pictured someone shorter, with thinning hair, thick spectacles, and a stern attitude. She got the hair right. The rest was off, replaced by a jovial smile and bright hazel eyes.

"Hello, Casey," Pastor Burgess said. "Thank you so much for agreeing to do this. Lydia wasn't a member here long, but most folks knew and loved her even before she joined our church."

Comforted by the pastor's presence, Casey managed a smile. "Thank you. It means a lot to me that you all took the time to remember Aunt Liddy like this."

He patted her arm and began introducing the guests until an elderly woman bent on capturing his attention happened by. Monah quickly assumed his responsibilities.

"That's Adele and Frank Finch. They own the grocery store downtown. Lydia used to cut Adele's hair," Monah said in her ear.

Casey smiled and shook their hands in turn.

"And that's Homer Burns, from the Cash-n-Carry. Remember him? His daughter Tracy married Lloyd Jacobs."

The names didn't mean much to Casey's fuddled

mind, but Monah's chatter kept her from having to talk.

Luke and Jack Kerrigan entered from the rear. She caught a glimpse of them, both dressed in black and sporting ties, the same sad look in their eyes.

Luke glanced up and saw her. He didn't smile, but warmth shone from his gaze. She drew in a deep breath. It was almost as if he'd wrapped her in a warm hug. She looked away.

Behind the Kerrigans, Mike Brockman entered. Monah gave a sharp intake of breath and lifted her hand to smooth her hair.

She's never been self-conscious before, Casey thought. She hid a knowing smile as Monah shifted from foot to foot while he approached.

"Hi, Mike," Monah said, a trifle breathlessly.

"Hi, Monah. Pastor Burgess." He turned to Casey and extended his hand. "It's good to see you again, Miss Alexander. I hate it has to be under these circumstances."

"Thank you. I appreciate your coming." She took his hand, surprised when he held on a tad longer than necessary.

"You still have my number, don't you? Feel free to call anytime, especially if you find out anything new about your aunt. I'm always available."

Casey glanced at Monah, who was staring at their hands. "Yes, I have it. Thank you, Officer."

He released her with a smile. "Call me Mike."

Beside them, Pastor Burgess glanced at his watch. "I see they're lighting candles. We must be getting close. I'd better go check on the accompanists."

"Is it time to start?" Casey whispered to Monah as Pastor Burgess and Officer Brockman excused themselves.

"Almost. Let's find a seat."

Monah led the way to a row of white chairs that a velvet banner proclaimed as reserved. After a moment, Luke and Jack joined them. Jack slid his arm around Casey's shoulder and gave her a squeeze before he took the seat next to her.

The scent of freshly baked brownies wafted from the kitchen. The women of the church intended to serve sandwiches after the service. Already, Casey heard them bustling about, scooping ice into cups, pouring tea.

Strange. One wall was all that separated the life and activity in there from the sorrow and death out here. She tugged a tissue from her purse and dabbed at her eyes. Waterproof mascara had to be the best invention since indoor plumbing.

"You all right?" Monah peered at her, her own eyes red with unshed tears.

"I'm fine. Hey, that picture by the guest book, do you know where it came from?"

"It's mine. I took it last October during the Fall Festival. Why?"

"It's beautiful. Do you think you could make me a copy?"

"No problem."

The strains of "Amazing Grace" stifled their conversation. Casey looked at Monah and lifted an eyebrow in question.

"After Lydia got saved, she said she'd never listen to the words of this hymn the same way again," Monah whispered. "I thought she'd like it."

A strange envy flooded Casey's heart. Monah knew a side of Aunt Liddy she would never see. She shook her head to rid herself of the thought and concentrated on another picture of Aunt Liddy, this one black-and-white, smiling at her from the platform. She looked beautiful in her favorite sweater, a scarf around her neck, and her hair swept back. Next to the picture, a bouquet of roses added a splash of color.

Roses.

Casey frowned. She'd meant to call Black's Floral after she found that receipt in Luke's truck. She risked a peek. He looked stoic, without a hint of dampness in his eyes. Jack, on the other hand, wept openly. Puzzled, Casey studied them for a moment. From the corner of her eye, she saw someone studying her, the heavy stare raising the hair on the back of her neck. She shifted her gaze to see the person's face, her fingers itching for the Post-its tucked inside her purse.

Mental note: attractive woman, medium height, slightly overweight, with short brown hair curling at the edges.

Who was she, and why did she seem so intent upon her? She blinked, checked her watch, and looked back. Still the woman stared. Goose bumps rose along her arms. Or was it. . .

Jack. The woman seemed to be eyeing Jack. Interesting.

"I'd like to welcome you all," Pastor Burgess began, pulling her thoughts away from the guests. His deep voice added a touch of dignity to the somber affair. He invited the guests to celebrate Aunt Liddy's life, the cheerful smile she brought to every gathering, the goodness of her heart. He touched on her passing, bringing a fresh flood of tears to Casey's eyes with his grace and tact. Behind her, muffled sniffles mingled with her own. Somehow, knowing she was not alone in her grief made her feel better.

"And so, let us remember what God said when events leave us wondering. Let us ponder His message and grab hold of His promises. He asks us to trust Him with all our hearts. Can we do that? Do we understand what it means to lean not on our own understanding?" Pastor Burgess shook his head. "That's hard to do sometimes, especially in trials such as this. But God wants us to acknowledge Him. He wants us to look to Him, even when life doesn't seem to make sense."

He dropped his gaze to Casey. "I've learned what it means to trust without asking why. No matter what hurts we've been dealt in the past, God is able to bring healing."

Her breath caught. She didn't have issues with trust, did she? She lowered her head while he ended the service, glad when the last note of the closing hymn faded and she could rise with the others and make her way to the kitchen, away from Pastor Burgess's probing words.

Good as the food smelled, Casey didn't taste a bite. It scraped down her throat like sandpaper. She needed air.

She wound her way to the back of the room and slid out the rear entrance. Thankfully, the rain had stopped, and only the fresh scent of damp earth remained. Ahead, a familiar figure was just leaving.

"Ross? Ross Derkson?"

The groundskeeper from the state park paused with his hand on the door of his car. "Yes?"

"I'm Casey Alexander. We met the other day."

He turned to face her. "I remember."

"I left an impression, huh?" Casey said, chagrined.

Ross laughed and looked her over from head to toe. "You could say that. How are you?"

"I'm fine, thanks. I'll be better after today."

He tossed a glance back at the church. "Yeah. I'm really sorry about all of this. The service was nice."

"Thank you." Suddenly at a loss, Casey shoved her hands into her pockets. "Listen, I was wondering, the meeting with Luke Kerrigan, was that planned?"

"Excuse me?" His eyebrows scrunched into a bushy line.

"Luke said you hired him as a consultant. Was it a spur-of-the-moment thing?"

"We tried to get together a couple of times, but the weather"—he shrugged and glanced up at the gray sky—"doesn't always cooperate."

"So Luke didn't suggest it at the last minute."

"No," Ross said, obviously baffled.

Casey backed away. "Okay. Thanks for your time."

He was still watching her when she reached the church door. She waved and ducked inside. *If he didn't think I was strange before, he certainly does now.*

"There you are. I searched all over for you. Are you okay?" Monah's round eyes looked even bigger behind the black glasses.

Ashamed of the worry she read on Monah's face, Casey nodded. "Yeah. Just getting a breather. It was pretty thick in there."

Monah smiled and grasped Casey's elbow. "Maybe I can make you feel better."

"What do you mean?"

"I'll show you." She led her back into the main room, where people gathered to eat and talk. "Remember when I told you that Lydia didn't have many enemies?"

Casey nodded.

"He was one of the few." She pointed to a tall thin man with intense eyes and a hawklike nose.

"Is that—?"

"Maxwell Novak," Monah finished.

"What's he doing here?"

"Drumming up business?"

Casey jerked her head to stare at her. "You've got to be kidding."

"You never know."

"Okay, what about her?" Casey pointed to the staring woman.

"Carol Hester?"

"Is that her name?"

"Uh-huh. She's Jack's assistant."

Oh, brother. An office romance? "Tell me what you know about her."

"Hello, ladies."

Both Monah and Casey jumped at the unexpected voice.

"Detective Rafferty." Casey clasped her hands behind her back, feeling a bit like a child caught stealing cookies.

Detective Rafferty peered at them, his gaze swinging from her to Monah. "I assume the two of you are staying out of trouble?"

A sound escaped Monah. Casey jumped in before she could speak. "Do you have news for me, Detective?"

Doubt lingered in Rafferty's eyes, but he nodded anyway. "We found Maxwell Novak's truck. It had a ding in the front bumper. Everything else checked out okay."

"A ding?" Her heart rate sped. "Does that mean you can arrest him?"

"For what? You didn't get a look at the driver, and Maxwell reported the truck stolen." He pulled a stick of gum from his pocket. Peppermint wafted from his fingers as he unwrapped it and stuck it in his mouth. "Also, I checked with Bob on your brake line. He saw a little wear, but from what you told me about the accident the day before, I'd say it could have happened anytime. Maybe some mice got to it—chewed up the line."

Casey crossed her arms. Brandy Purcell never took no for an answer. Neither would she.

"What about fingerprints?"

Exasperation mottled Rafferty's expression. He ran his hand around the collar of his white button-down shirt. "Fingerprints."

"Did you see if you could lift any prints from Mr. Novak's truck, or my brake line for that matter?"

Lift prints. Casey bit back a smile. She sounded like a real sleuth straight out of the True Life Detective series. Next to her, Monah stared in open amazement.

"No, Miss Alexander. We didn't manage to 'lift' any prints."

"Well, I'm available if you need someone with their own fingerprinting kit. I learned how to do it from studying Brandy Purcell."

Rafferty's eyebrows shot upward. "You have your own fingerprinting kit?"

"You read Brandy Purcell?" Monah added.

"Yes, I do, and yes, I do."

Monah looked at Rafferty, who shook his head.

Rafferty shoved his hand deep into his pocket, a smirk playing at his lips. At his hip, a revolver gleamed. "I'll keep that in mind. . .next time I need somebody to help me lift fingerprints."

"I'm glad to help, Detective," Casey said as Rafferty excused himself and sauntered away.

"When did you start reading Brandy Purcell?"

Casey cast a sidelong glance at Monah.

She pushed her glasses farther up her nose and poked Casey's elbow. "Well?"

From the corner of her eye, a hint of movement caught Casey's attention. "Awhile ago." She shifted to peer over Monah's shoulder. A scrap of black fluttered and disappeared around the corner. "I'll be right back."

"Where are you going?"

She ignored Monah's question and started down the hall. Her pace increased as, once again, the figure slipped through a doorway before she could get a good look.

What was it about the person that looked so familiar? The park, the night she was attacked!

She broke into a run. "Hey, wait up. Excuse me. Could I talk to you a moment?"

Unbalanced by her heels, she paused long enough to rip them from her feet before barreling down the hall.

"I said—"

Whumph.

She ran headlong into a man's chest. . .hard. It knocked the breath from her lungs. She stumbled, almost fell, and then the man caught her by the arms.

"Casey? Is that you, sweetheart? Where are you going?"

She couldn't believe her eyes. She wanted to run, wanted to cry. Instead, she took a deep breath and stared up into the face of the father she only knew from her parents' wedding photo.

8

After Pastor Burgess's soothing service concluded, Luke joined the ranks of people standing in line for food. One of the women serving lunch plunked half a pimento cheese sandwich on his plate. Ugh. Somebody always brought that stuff. He nodded politely to a couple of blue-haired members of the hostess committee who exclaimed over the landscaping he did for the church. He munched on a carrot, scanning the room for signs of Casey's blond head.

After ten minutes of parrying questions by curious parishioners, he'd had enough.

"Sorry, ladies." He dropped his paper plate into the trash can along with his cup and napkin. "Wish I could stay and chat. . ."

"Don't you worry." The shorter of the two women patted his arm. "I'm sure you want to get back to your father. The poor dear is having an awful time of it."

He glanced at his dad. The tie hung loose around his neck. His eyes watered, the tears spilling into the silk handkerchief pressed to his nose, but that was to be expected. He and Lydia had been friends as long as Luke could remember.

A familiar question surfaced in Luke's mind. Were they more than just friends? Many times while growing up, he felt his dad loved Lydia more than him. Perhaps that accounted for the emotional distance between them. He shoved the thought aside and crossed the room, ignoring the whispered remarks of the two old women who bent their heads together the moment they thought he was out of earshot.

"How you doing, Dad?"

Jack Kerrigan swiped the handkerchief across his nose one last time before shoving it into his pocket. His shoulders drooped. "I don't know, Luke. I just don't know."

His gaze fell from his father's red eyes. He hated seeing him this way. It was so unlike him to express emotion. "Can I get you something, maybe a drink from the kitchen?" He started that way, but his dad stopped him with a shake of his head.

"I'd rather you see to Casey. I'd do it myself. . ." He trailed off, his shoulders rising in a helpless shrug. "I'm not much good to anyone right now."

Luke took a quick look around the room. Still no Casey.

"She went that way." His dad pointed to the back. "Don't worry about me. I'll be fine, eventually. I've still got you. Casey hasn't got anyone." His voice thickened, and he fished out the handkerchief once more. "Take care of Lydia's niece for me, would you?" He spun before Luke could protest and hurried out the exit into the parking lot.

Luke headed down the hall. Keeping an eye on Casey was like trying to hold a wiggly puppy. She'd already disappeared on him once, and now he'd lost sight of her again. He only wanted to make sure she made it through the day okay. Losing someone you loved was excruciating.

The vision of her in a man's arms at the end of the hall stopped him cold. A knot formed in his stomach. Not much taller than she was, the gentleman wore an expensive-looking suit.

When she struggled and shoved away, Luke sped to her side.

"Casey? Everything okay?"

Without a word, she took hold of his elbow and slipped around behind him. Luke's blood surged with a desire to protect her. Even though the man in front of him looked familiar and was old enough to be his father, Luke would do whatever it took to keep Casey safe.

"Can I help you?"

The older man frowned and tried to step past him. Luke kept himself between the two. The man gave a helpless gesture.

"Casey, sweetheart, I just want to talk."

Sweetheart?

Luke turned to look at her. Huge tears spilled from her eyes. She pointed her shaking finger at the man.

"Don't. . .you dare. . .call me that. You lost the right to call me sweetheart the day you left Mom and me."

She choked on the last word as she turned and ran away.

Casey's father. The realization hit him like a blast of ice water. He moved to go after her, but the hand grasping his arm stopped him. He jerked away.

"Wait, young man."

Luke glanced down the hall. No sign of Casey. . . again. He faced the man he'd only seen in Lydia's photo album. The hard eyes he expected weren't there. Instead, he found a hopeless expression.

Mr. Alexander extended his hand. "I'm Richard Alexander. You a friend of Casey's?"

Luke accepted the handshake. *Soft. No calluses.* "I'd like to think so."

"Good. Maybe you can help me."

He lifted an eyebrow, waiting.

"I came here hoping to reconcile with my daughter. When I heard about Lydia's death, I knew Casey would come. I thought this might be the best chance I had of righting all my past wrongs."

While he spoke, Mr. Alexander crossed his arms, and his voice deepened. The impression he gave grated on Luke even though his eyes pleaded for understanding.

"Luke?"

Monah's interruption couldn't have come at a better time. He needed a minute to think about what Mr. Alexander was saying.

"Luke Kerrigan?"

Caught off guard by the man's use of his name, Luke swung to peer at him. "How'd you know my name?"

The man blinked twice and licked his lips. "I met your dad several years back."

Luke nodded, unease rolling through him. "Uh, if you'll excuse me, I'm going to see what Monah needs."

"Sure. Maybe we can get together later."

Luke took Monah by the arm and propelled her down the hall. He didn't turn her loose until they were back in the main room. She pulled free and peered up at him.

"What's going on? Who was that man?"

"Casey's dad."

"Really?" Monah peeked back down the hall. "Lydia told me a little about that situation. Does Casey know he's here?"

"Yeah. And she ran out of here in tears."

"Because of him or Lydia?"

"Had to be her dad. Today of all days. He sure picked the wrong time to do this."

"I'll check on her later. In the meantime, I was

wondering how you were doing." Monah put her arm around his waist. "This has to be hard on you, too. Lydia's memorial on the anniversary of your mom's death. That's got to be rough."

Just hearing the words sent a shaft of pain through his heart. *God has a plan and purpose,* he reminded himself. "Yeah. But that was over twenty years ago. This is all fresh for Casey. And right now, she's my main concern. We at least need to call her."

Mr. Alexander entered, and his head swiveled back and forth as he glanced around the room. Luke took Monah by the arm. "Let's find a quiet place to make the call." *Anywhere but near Casey's dad.* A reconciliation between father and daughter would be just what Lydia wanted, but until Casey was ready for it, Luke planned to avoid doing anything that might widen the gap he fought to remove.

Bitterness clouded Casey's vision. She scrubbed the tears from her cheeks and clenched the steering wheel tighter. Who did her father think he was, anyway? Showing up at Aunt Liddy's memorial service, of all places. Never mind he was her brother. That never mattered before. What could he possibly want after all these years?

She drummed her fingers against her thigh, impatient for the light to change. When it finally did, she turned the corner and sped up the hill toward the highway.

The porch lights of Aunt Liddy's house beckoned, a welcome sight against the gloom caused by the overcast sky. Maybe she wouldn't have to deal with a flood of well-meaning phone calls and could just curl up on the couch.

Except she hadn't turned on the porch lights. The thought struck her as she rolled to a stop in the driveway. They came on by themselves when someone passed by the sensor. Goose bumps pricked her skin.

Get a grip, Case. It was probably a squirrel or something.

A really, really big squirrel, in order to trip the sensor. She grimaced and yanked open the door handle. Her imagination was getting out of hand lately. Time to put down the Brandy Purcell books and read something a little lighter. Like *Macbeth*.

Still, she eased the car door closed and tiptoed toward the steps. Halfway up, lingering thunder nearly sent her diving off the porch. She took a deep breath, collected herself, and walked the rest of the way.

The knob turned effortlessly in her hand. Had she locked it? She couldn't remember. Her thoughts had been in a haze before the service. She pushed open the door, leaving it ajar in case she needed to beat a hasty retreat.

This was stupid. How many times had she shouted out in frustration when Brandy Purcell walked into certain danger, her long hair swinging, eyes alight with bravery? Don't do it, Brandy. Don't go in there! And here she was, *step*, doing exactly the same thing. *Step, step, swallow.*

Time to find a weapon. She grabbed an umbrella from the stand next to the door and moved down the hall toward the den. The leftover rain clouds made it dark inside. Her eyes strained to see.

Her fingers itched to find the power switch, but she knew if an intruder did lurk inside, the light would scare the person away.

So she crept forward, scarcely daring to draw a breath, until—

A shadowy figure hunched over the desk in Aunt Liddy's den, made all the more menacing by the hat, dark clothes, and gloves that covered the person from head to toe. Her stomach lurched. Suddenly the umbrella didn't seem like such a good idea. She inched backward.

Creak.

How could one loose floorboard sound so deafening? She froze, her heart hammering. Saliva flooded her mouth. Sweat dampened her palms.

The figure whirled and tossed a sheaf of papers at her face, blinding her.

Casey shrieked and started swinging. For all the good it did. She found only air, paper, air. And Aunt Liddy's Tiffany lamp. It crashed to floor. She fumbled for the light switch and snapped it on.

The room was a mess. Papers fluttered to the floor. Glass lay everywhere. The desk drawers tilted haphazardly at odd angles. Across the room, a window stood half open. And the mysterious figure was nowhere to be found.

9

Casey paced up and down the hall, casting a glance at her watch and another into the den as she strode past. A slight breeze stirred the curtains and sent chills over her skin. The window the figure had disappeared through stared at her like a big blank eye. Officer Brockman said not to touch anything.

Where is he, anyway?

The soft purr of an engine sounded outside. She raced to the front and threw open the door. "In here."

Mike Brockman, still dressed in his black suit and tie, climbed out of his car and hurried up the sidewalk. "Are you all right? I came as soon as you called."

"I'm fine." She peered over his shoulder. "Where's Detective Rafferty?"

"He's. . .uh. . . It's Saturday, and. . ." He tugged at his tie. "Well, he goes to visit his wife every week. I came alone."

Strange for him to act so uncomfortable. Casey raised an eyebrow. "He visits her? Is she sick or something? I didn't even realize he was married."

"Yeah, twenty-five years or something like that. She got sick. . .you know"—he pointed at his head—"and since he couldn't take care of her, he put her in a home over in Marlborough. He never misses a visit."

Every week for twenty-five years? What a surprise. She didn't figure Rafferty for the sensitive type.

She shook her head. "Okay, I'll show you where I found the intruder. This way." She led him down the hall.

"That the desk?"

"Uh-huh." She picked up a tackle-box-sized container from off the floor. "I got my fingerprinting kit out of the car in case you needed it."

He froze. "Fingerprinting kit? I thought you said the intruder wore gloves."

"He did."

"He?"

"Or she."

Officer Brockman's eyes narrowed. "You didn't touch anything, did you?"

She frowned. "Of course not. I would never disturb the scene of a crime. But you might dust the drawer pulls, just in case the person got careless."

A look of puzzlement creased his forehead. "How come you know so much about police work?"

"Casey? Mike? Where are you guys?" Monah appeared, her long hair damp and windblown, her glasses slightly askew. She jerked her thumb toward the front. "I saw Mike's car in the driveway, and the door was open, so—" She stopped and stared into the den. "What happened?"

Casey hurried to her side. "Hi, Monah. I'm glad you're here. You'll never believe—"

"Please don't come any closer." Officer Brockman held out a warning hand. "I'd rather you didn't enter until I've had a chance to look everything over."

"Look what over? What happened?" When Brockman refused to answer, Monah turned to Casey.

"I found an intruder in the house when I got back from the service," Casey said. "The person was going through Aunt Liddy's desk."

"An intruder! Are you okay?"

"Yeah, I'm fine. He fled as soon as I threatened him with my umbrella."

Monah's mouth dropped, and her glasses slid down her nose. "I'm not even going to ask."

"Any idea what the person was looking for?" Brockman riffled through some of the papers scattered over the floor.

"None."

Monah leaned to Casey's ear. "Does he know about the other time? In the park?"

"No," Casey whispered back.

"Do you think it was the same person?"

"No idea. I didn't see either one long enough to tell."

Brockman rose and went to the desk. "Is anything missing, as far as you can tell?"

"I don't know. You told me not to touch anything."

She returned an innocent stare when he raised his eyebrows. He sighed and went to check the window.

"Maybe you should tell him."

Adamant, Casey shook her head. "Not yet."

"Why not?"

She crossed her arms. She didn't trust anybody right now; that was why not. And Brockman. . . Something just didn't sit right.

She cast a sidelong glance at Monah. "What are you doing here, anyway?"

"Luke and I wanted to make sure you were okay. He said he was gonna call, but I told him I'd stop by instead."

"This belong to you?" Brockman held up a necklace, its delicate gold chain and diamond pendant glistening.

Casey walked to him and leaned close. "It belonged to

Aunt Liddy. Where did you find it?"

Brockman pointed. "Top drawer. The intruder had to have seen it."

She tapped her temple. "Why didn't he take it?"

"Good question." He laid it aside. "I think we'd better do a quick check through the rest of the house." He motioned toward the hall, and Casey signaled Monah.

"Go ahead," Monah said, pulling her cell phone from her jacket pocket. "I've got a call to make."

The downstairs and kitchen revealed no trace of the intruder. Upstairs, the beds were neatly made and the windows all locked. Nothing appeared to be missing.

"So what was he looking for in the desk?" Casey said as they made their way back to the den.

Brockman shrugged. "How big did you say this person was?"

Casey tugged a yellow Post-it Note out of her pocket. "I couldn't tell his height. He was bent over. Weight looked to be about 170 pounds." She paused and peered at him. "But he was wearing bulky clothing. He may have been thinner."

"Less would mean a pretty small guy." Brockman took the last step and turned to go into the den where Monah waited.

Monah flipped her phone closed. "So?"

Casey shook her head. "What are you saying, Officer? You think the intruder was a woman?"

"Actually," Brockman said, scratching his head, "I'm thinking more like a kid."

"A kid? Why?"

Monah moved alongside Casey, her large eyes rounder than normal behind the black frames. "Yeah, why?"

"The desk." Brockman went over to it. "Nothing of value is missing. I'm thinking the intruder was looking for money, possibly even credit card receipts or bank accounts so they could steal the numbers. The rate of teenaged offenders is on the rise, and this would be exactly the kind of crime they'd commit. Another thing, the memorial service was publicized. This happens a lot—people come home from funerals and find their homes have been burglarized."

Monah elbowed Casey in the ribs. "Tell him."

He lifted his head and frowned. "Tell me what?"

Casey glared at Monah. "Nothing. So you think this is an isolated event?"

"That would be my guess," he said, "though I'd stay on my guard if I were you. Keep an eye out for anything unusual. Call me if you discover anything we overlooked." He moved to the door.

"I'll walk you out." Monah pivoted to hide her smile from him and gestured to Casey with her finger. *I'll be right back,* she mouthed and pointed toward the door.

Casey nodded then eyed the room with a sigh. The mess would take all night to clean up. She bent to grab one of the discarded pages—a garbage receipt from several months ago. Under that lay an old light bill. Maybe Officer Brockman was right.

The bright red box containing her fingerprinting equipment beckoned to her from the doorway. She retrieved it and grabbed a pair of latex gloves out of one of its drawers. Once she wrestled them on, she picked up a brush and the vial filled with volcanic ash. Using small, circular motions, she dusted each of the desk handles. The moisture-resistant adhesive she used to lift the prints was covered with partial images, all distorted by the uneven surface of the handles.

Monah reentered the room. "He's gone."

"Too bad. Methinks you wouldn't have minded him hanging around."

Monah's quick blush spoke volumes. "Uh, he's all right. Whatcha doin'?"

"Trying to get the intruder's fingerprint."

"You dusted the desk handles?"

"Yeah."

"You won't get a good print off those. It has to be a smooth, nonporous surface. Did you try the desktop?"

Casey held out a second pair of gloves. "Not yet. You want to help?"

Excitement lit Monah's face. "Sure."

A thorough dusting of the desk, window, and front door revealed nothing more than smudges. They gave up and went back to tidy the den.

Monah took a sheet of paper from Casey's hand. "What you got here?"

"Old statements." She ran her hand through her hair and picked her way across the room.

Monah lifted the broken lamp and let it dangle from the cord. "What happened to this?"

"The umbrella."

"Oh." She grabbed the trash can from beside the desk and dropped the lamp inside. "Got a broom?"

Casey scooped up a handful of papers and deposited them next to the lamp. "Hall closet."

They worked for several moments, Casey scooping, sorting, Monah sweeping broken glass. When she finished, she replaced the broom and set about helping Casey.

Casey passed her a stack. "Can you look through that? See if there's anything important in there."

"Sure." Monah plopped cross-legged on the floor. Before long, they had two piles in front of them, one for trash, one to be looked over later.

"Hey, Casey?"

She kept sorting. "Yeah?"

"Look at this."

Monah held several pages in her hand. Across the top was emblazoned LAST WILL AND TESTAMENT.

"Is that—?" She took the document, her hands shaking.

"Lydia's will," Monah whispered.

Casey broke the hush. "Should we read it?"

Tires squealed, startling them both. Casey scrambled upright and ran to the window. A familiar black truck dominated the driveway. She turned to Monah.

"How did he—?"

Monah blew out a breath. "I called. I figured he'd want to know."

"You what?"

"Casey! Monah!"

"You'd better answer that," Monah said. "He sounds about ready to come through the walls."

Luke pounded so hard, Casey half expected the door to crash open. She shoved the will at Monah and hurried down the hall.

The knob shook as, once again, Luke pounded. Casey managed to wriggle it open a second before he burst through.

He grabbed her arms. "Are you all right?"

"I'm fine—"

He glanced over her shoulder. "Monah?"

"Right here." She appeared in the doorway, a big smile on her lips. "Hi, Luke."

"What happened?" he demanded. His hair was mussed, and his face glowed red.

Heart thumping, Casey realized Luke still held her arms and was staring at her, his dark green eyes intense and filled with. . .what? Her insides turned to liquid. She couldn't be attracted to him. He might be a killer. "I. . .I. . .there. . ."

One hand rose to touch her cheek. "You're not hurt, are you?"

The whispered question sent flames licking through her veins. Her mouth went dry. She couldn't even speak with him so close, his touch warm upon her skin, his aftershave tickling her nose. She shook her head.

He let out a breath, his broad shoulders relaxing a bit beneath the white tailored shirt he wore. His hands fell away.

Her lungs worked again. "Someone broke in while we were at the church. I caught them going through Aunt Liddy's desk."

"Anything missing?"

"I don't think so. Monah and I are sorting everything out now."

He looked up. "I'm glad you're here, Monah. Thanks for calling."

She pushed her glasses up her nose and shrugged. "No problem. You made record time." She directed a pointed glance at her watch and then ducked through the door, a chuckle floating down the hall.

"You didn't have to come. But I'm glad you did,"

Casey added hastily. She hugged her middle and bit her bottom lip.

"Casey. . ." He leaned closer.

When she dared look up, his face was only inches from hers. "Yes?"

"You. . ."

Tempted to let her eyelids drift close, she felt herself rising onto her tiptoes, her body straining to meet him. "Uh-huh?"

". . .need better locks."

"What?" Her eyes snapped open.

He cleared his throat and moved back a step. "To keep them from breaking in here again. I think you should install some dead bolts, maybe get some security bars for the windowsills when you're not using them. The windows, I mean."

Bewildered, she glanced around the room. "I suppose so." What had he been about to say? Somehow, she knew he'd changed his mind before voicing it. "Luke—"

"I'll pick them up. Will you be okay by yourself for a little bit?"

"Monah's here."

"Oh yeah. Right. I'll be back soon, then. Lock the door anyway."

She nodded. He strode out.

Tick, tick, tick. Aunt Liddy's grandfather clock sounded monstrous in the empty hallway. She glanced at it. Seven o'clock. Gradually her heart rate returned to normal, but the disappointment that Luke hadn't kissed her took longer to fade. She rejoined Monah on the floor in the den.

"Where's Luke?"

"He went to get locks."

"Good idea." Monah paused, her head tilted like a little bird. "Are you okay? You look frazzled."

Casey smoothed her hair, licked her lips. "I'm all right. Where were we?"

Patting the sheets of paper around her, Monah found the ones she wanted and held them up. "The will. Do we or don't we?" Her eyes widened. "I'm sorry, Casey. Maybe you'd like to be alone while you read it?"

"No way. I can use the support." She took the document. Tears filled her eyes as she read the first few words aloud. " 'I, Lydia Claude Alexander, residing at Pine Mills, Massachusetts, being of sound mind, do hereby declare this instrument to be my last will and testament.' " She sniffed and handed it to Monah. "Would you?"

"Sure," she said softly.

Aunt Liddy bequeathed almost everything to Casey, just as Jack said. *Almost everything.*

Casey's nails pinched circles into her palms. "Could you read that last part again?"

"The part about Luke?"

"Yeah. Read it again."

Monah ran her finger over the document. " 'To my beloved brother, Richard, I leave the antique gun once owned by John Quincy Adams.' " She looked up. "That's really cool by the way. Ah, here it is. 'I give all the rest and residue of my estate to my dear friend Luke Andrew Kerrigan. I pray that in a small way, this recompenses all that I owe you.' "

Monah's glasses had slid to the tip of her nose while she read. She pushed them back and lifted a questioning eyebrow. "What does she owe him?"

"I don't know."

"Maybe some kind of debt?"

Distrust curdled in the pit of Casey's stomach. "Does it say how much she left him?"

She flipped the page, peering through her glasses at the fine print. "Fifty thousand. That's some debt."

"Let me see that." Casey grabbed the document. "Monah, that's a lot of money."

"I'll say."

"Enough to kill for?"

Monah's mouth dropped open, and shock registered in her brown eyes. "You don't think Luke killed Lydia in order to get his inheritance!"

"People have killed for less."

"Not Luke." Monah grabbed her shoulders. "You've got to get over this distrust you have of him. It's almost like you're hoping he's the bad guy. Why would you do that? Why don't you want him to get close to you?"

Why don't I? Her toes curled inside her socks. *Why am I attracted to him one moment and convinced he's guilty the next?*

Tires crunched in the driveway, but neither one jumped up.

Casey tensed, her ears straining, fingers twitching, listening for the sound of the doorbell.

Luke waited at the door, moisture from his palms soaking into the paper bag from the hardware store. Maybe it wasn't from nerves. Maybe the hot pizza box he balanced on his fist and forearm caused the sweat.

He'd made a fool of himself with Casey earlier. What would she have done if he'd actually kissed her? A huge part of him ached to find out. But could he risk a slap on the face? Besides, the moment was gone, just like the words he'd almost said.

Footsteps from the other side of the door brought him back to the present just before it swung open. Casey stood there looking. . .

She turned away before he could figure out the expression on her face. What possibly could have happened in the short time he'd been away?

The door remained wide open, leaving him to fend for himself. He entered, making sure the toolbox didn't hit the jamb, and kicked the door closed. Monah stood at the office, her eyes glued to the pizza box. Luke brushed past, setting the toolbox on the floor and the pizza on the desk.

"I figured no one thought to cook, so I called Jake's. Only the best for my two girls."

Casey, standing as far from him as the room allowed, gave a quiet snort. Skewered. That was the only word he could think of to describe what her eyes did to him.

Monah patted him on the arm. "Very thoughtful, Luke, but I can't stay." She never made it out of the room. Casey snagged her arm as she passed.

Luke didn't catch much of the animated exchange going on between them, but he did hear Monah say the words "trust" and "no way." Great. Back to square one. Casey still suspected him.

Monah gave Casey a quick hug and headed back toward him. She flipped open the pizza box and grabbed a slice. "You know how I hate to eat and run, but I don't mind eating on the run." She gave him a wink. "You two have fun." She said the last words with a grin and dancing Groucho Marx eyebrows before disappearing out the door.

Luke fingered the stacks of papers on the desk. "Find anything that might help solve the crime?"

"Which crime would that be, Luke?"

He ignored the dig, his gaze landing on the words LAST WILL AND TESTAMENT. "You found Lydia's will?"

Casey scooted across the room and snatched the papers from his grasp. "You aren't supposed to read that, though I'm sure you already know you're in it."

He swallowed hard, his chest burning. "I'm in her will?"

"Don't act like you didn't know." She crossed her arms and leaned her hip against the desk. "Just how bad did you need the money?"

In an instant, everything became clear. Irritation started in his gut and threatened to blow off the top of his head.

"For Pete's sake, Casey, when are you going to get it through that pretty blond head of yours that I would never hurt Lydia?"

Her pad of Post-it Notes sat on the desk. He grabbed a pen out of the holder and wrote, "Luke didn't kill Aunt Lydia."

"Here," he said as he peeled off the note and stuck it to her forehead, "add this to your collection." He picked up his toolbox and the bag of locks. "Enjoy the pizza. I've got work to do."

Disappointment in Casey still smoldered inside him fifteen minutes later. He turned the screw so tight it stripped. The scent of tomato sauce, pepperoni, and cheese drifted over his shoulder. Casey set the plate down and squatted next to him.

"I'm sorry." Her eyes mirrored her words. She motioned to the lock. "Can I help?"

He wished he could have known her thoughts, whatever they were that brought her to him. But no matter. He'd make the most of the warmth that now emanated from her.

"Well, if you can turn screws as fast as you drive, we'll be done in no time."

A slow smile crept across her face. She gave him a shove. "I'm not that bad."

"Oh, so you admit you're a little bad?" They shared a laugh. "Grab that screwdriver. My fingers are going numb."

In minutes, the front door had a new dead bolt. He headed for the den. "I bought these fancy new locks for the windows. Justin, the guy at the hardware store, told me he installed them at his mom's house and they work great."

"Sounds good. How can I help?"

An hour later, after chatting about everything from rosebushes to Web sites, they knelt at the last window on the bottom floor. Luke held out his hand for another lock. "You know, I tried to talk Lydia into doing this when I helped her hide that key, her being out here alone and all. She wanted nothing to do with it. Said she'd been fine all these years without fancy locks."

Casey set the screws on the sill, working them around with the tip of her finger. "You really did love Aunt Liddy, didn't you?"

He looked her right in the eyes. "Absolutely. She was

the mom I never had. Stepped in when Mom died and never stepped out, until now. I could have been her son, the way she treated me." He wanted to say more, but the words wouldn't come. Grief twisted his stomach. He turned to the window.

Casey sat with her back against the wall. "What happened to your mom? I don't think I ever heard the story."

Another difficult topic, but at least the hurt wasn't as fresh as losing Lydia. He marked where the screws went and drilled the first one home. The sawdust smell was familiar, unchanging. Something he could draw strength from. "She died in a car wreck. Hit-and-run."

"I'm sorry. Did they ever find out who did it?"

"Nope. Dad said Rafferty was the cop on duty that night. He's the one who found me and called for an ambulance."

She gave a soft gasp. "You were in the accident with your mom? Were you hurt?"

"No. She had me in a car seat in the back." He drilled in the last screw and sat on the floor beside her. "From what Dad told me, they never could find enough evidence to prove who did it. They think it might have been someone from out of town, and they just kept going."

His dad's face came to mind, and he wondered once more if the accident had caused the distance between them. Maybe Dad blamed him for losing his wife. He'd never managed to ask him that question, unsure if he wanted to hear the answer.

Casey leaned over and bumped him with her shoulder. "You disappeared on me. You okay?"

Arms propped on his knees, he rubbed a piece of

wood from his fingers and looked at her, glad to see that no fear shone from her clear blue gaze, no distrust or suspicion. He stood and offered his hand. "You feel like some pizza?"

She accepted, her small hand warm in his, and allowed him to help her up. "No, I feel like an idiot. . .for ever thinking you could have killed Aunt Liddy." She gave his hand a squeeze before letting it go.

He headed for the pizza, his stomach demanding sustenance. "So what changed your mind?"

She cast him a lopsided grin. "I went back over my notes. Very compelling on your behalf, especially the last one."

He chuckled but stopped when she jabbed him in the ribs and held her finger up in front of him.

"But I give you fair warning, mister. Hands off my Post-its." Her other hand went to her heart. "I about went into shock when you started writing on my pad."

He grabbed her finger and shook it. *Lord, but she's cute.* "Deal."

10

Long after Luke left, Casey paced the house, her stomach in knots, Monah's words playing in her head.

"Why don't you want him to get close to you?"

Much as she hated to admit it, Monah was right. Part of her sensed her heart could safely trust him, and part of her wanted to turn tail and run. Why?

She paused and glanced up at the ceiling. "A little help here?"

No answer echoed back. She gave a snort and resumed her pacing. After another ten minutes of futile wandering, she plopped into the chair next to the fireplace and covered her face with her hands. This was ridiculous. Not only was she no closer to solving Aunt Liddy's murder, but she'd wasted an entire evening thinking of nothing but Luke. She needed to focus.

Aunt Liddy's collection of novels lined the bookshelves next to the fireplace. Among them were the Brandy Purcell books Casey had sent her as gifts. One in particular caught her eye. *Broken Dreams?* She snatched the volume off the shelf. She didn't think the latest in the True Life Detective series had even been released yet.

She smiled. A Brandy Purcell mystery was just what she needed to get back on track and thinking like a detective. She carried the book to the sofa and curled up with the afghan over her legs and a plump pillow behind her head, prepared to spend the night deep inside the pages.

Instead, she woke early the next morning with a splitting headache and eyes swollen from crying.

Who would've believed it? Newly was dead.

The thought brought a fountain of fresh tears. Brandy's partner and unofficial crime dog. . .dead. In chapter 10, a deranged gunman intent on killing Brandy stormed into her office waving a rifle. Always alert, always faithful, Newly jumped up to protect his mistress, taking a stray bullet for his loyalty. Casey's heart broke right along with Brandy's as her dearest friend drew his last breath.

She snatched a tissue out of the box and swabbed away the red-hot tears. Oh, if only Brandy had seen the gunman coming. If only—

The ringing of the doorbell kept her from finishing the thought. She looked at the clock. Seven thirty-five. Through the leaded pane, she saw Monah's figure outlined.

"Coming." She plucked another tissue from the box and trudged to the door.

"Hey—oh, sweetie!" Monah wrapped her in a hug the moment Casey opened up. "I knew I should have checked on you again. I'm so sorry. Did you have a rough night?"

She nodded.

"Do you want to talk about it?"

"I don't know if I can."

"Of course you can." Monah shut the door and took her elbow. "Let's go inside and sit down. Have you made coffee yet?"

A weak shake was all Casey could manage due to the pounding in her head. She let Monah lead her to the kitchen and pull all the stuff for coffee out of the cupboard.

"So what happened? Was it the will?"

She dropped into a chair at the table. Her head throbbed,

and gunk clogged her sinuses. "Huh?"

"Which is fine, you know. I can understand your emotions getting the better of you after the day you had. I mean, first the memorial service, then your dad showing up. And as if that weren't enough, your house got broken into. Who wouldn't be an emotional wreck?"

Monah could be a regular Chatty Cathy once she got rolling. She turned on the faucet, her hands talking almost as fast as her lips while she filled the carafe, dumped grounds in the filter, and set the timer.

"That was some nerve of your dad, by the way. Did he say what he wanted? 'Cause I gotta tell ya, half the town was shocked to see him after so many years. You never saw news spread so fast. I'm surprised your phone didn't ring off the hook. Of course, it helped that he decided to spend the night in town. Most folks probably just called Mabel, who owns the bed-and-breakfast on Park Street, and asked her what he was doing here. Not that she'd know, mind you. So what was it?"

She flopped into a chair next to Casey's and peered at her, brown eyes soft with concern.

Casey hiccupped and shrugged. "It was Newly."

Blank-eyed, Monah tilted her head and cocked an eyebrow. "Huh?"

"Brandy's crime dog. He. . . Oh, Monah! He's dead."

Ice plunked from the automatic maker into the freezer tray. The soft hum of the lights and gurgling of the coffeemaker grew in volume. Finally, Monah spoke. "That's why you were crying?"

"Uh-huh. I would have finished the book to find out what happens, except that I was so upset about Newly, I fell asleep crying."

"Er. . .let me get this straight." Monah pushed her glasses into place and waved her finger in the air. "After everything that happened yesterday, the thing that made you fall to pieces was a dog?"

Casey hesitated. Monah couldn't have looked more shocked. "It wasn't just any dog, Monah. It was Ne–w–ly." She stretched the word, as if by emphasizing it she could make her understand.

Blink, blink. Monah's eyes widened like a cartoon character's behind the thick glasses. "You know what you need?"

"What?" The restless stirring of Casey's hands stilled.

"Prayer. Lots of it." Monah rose and pulled her from the chair. "Get dressed. You're coming to church."

"But—"

"No buts. It's what Lydia would have wanted."

Unable to argue with that reasoning, Casey shuffled upstairs. In less than forty minutes, she'd showered, dressed, and pulled her blow-dried hair into a loose ponytail. It wasn't her most attractive look, but it would do.

Back in the kitchen, Monah handed her a travel mug filled with coffee. "Hope you weren't expecting breakfast."

"This'll do." Casey took a sip and followed her out the door, careful to lock the new dead bolt she and Luke had installed. The caffeine did wonders for her headache. By the time they arrived at the church, her eyes no longer felt ready to pop out of her head, and that, combined with the powder and mascara she'd applied in the car, gave her the confidence to proceed inside with a smile.

It was short-lived.

Her father looked up at her from the back row, his dark eyes hopeful. Fresh anger filled her. She stormed past him, ignoring his outstretched hand, and sat down in a pew near the front. Good thing they arrived early. The extra time and soft music floating from the piano helped calm her nerves.

"Welcome, Casey. I'm glad to see you here this morning." Pastor Burgess paused alongside their pew and offered his hand first to her then to Monah.

"Thank you, Pastor," Casey said.

"Good morning, Pastor," Monah added.

Once Pastor Burgess reached the podium, he wasted no time going over the announcements. "Lastly," he said, "I'd like to remind you all that Alma Harris's mother, Martha, is still laid up from the fall she took last week. We'll continue praying for her. Are there any other requests this morning?"

Several hands went up. Casey listened to pleas for jobs, health, unsaved family members, even prayers of comfort for those who had lost loved ones. Like her. She clenched her fists in her lap.

Pastor Burgess started praying, and Casey bowed her head with the others. Afterward, she sat back and enjoyed the pastor's sermon on love and forgiveness, but it was the hymn they closed with that invaded her thoughts and refused to leave. "Trust and Obey."

Why did everything seem to be pointing her toward trust? Trust who, for goodness' sake? She fidgeted in discomfort, avoiding the cross glowing above the baptistery.

Monah plunked the hymnal into the rack behind the pew. "How 'bout lunch? Fred's Diner has an awesome corned beef sandwich. It's just around the corner. You don't have plans, do you?" She rose.

Casey followed her out, exchanging greetings with several members on her way to the parking lot. Thankfully, her father was nowhere to be seen, but Luke was. She flushed as his warm gaze met hers. Oh, but he looked good enough to eat. Her stomach rumbled. "Well, I kinda have something I need to take care of, but it can wait."

Monah glanced at her over the hood of her car, her eyes questioning.

"The gun."

"Oh." She tugged a pair of sunglasses out of her purse and clipped them onto her eyeglasses. "I can help you look if you want."

Casey accepted the offer as they climbed into the car and set off down the road. "I'm hoping once I give the gun to him, I can put him out of my life forever."

"Are you sure that's what you want?" Monah pulled into Fred's and parked.

"Positive." She shut the door a little harder than necessary. Monah directed a sympathetic look at her that warmed Casey's heart.

Fred's Diner was a mix of quiet country and Wild West rodeo. Checkered cloths adorned the tables. Pictures of rodeo cowboys Tuff Hedeman and Cody Lambert hung on the walls. Patrons occupied half the tables, and they all looked up with interest when the young women entered. Several called a greeting to Monah, who waved back. The waitress led them to a booth, plunked down two menus, and took their drink order.

"So tell me what you know so far," Monah said while they waited for their iced teas to arrive.

"About Aunt Liddy's case?"

She nodded.

"Well. . ." Casey grabbed a stack of Post-its from her purse and spread them over the table. "Whoever killed her is still after something. That's why they broke into the house and went through her desk."

"I take it you don't buy the teenaged crime rate thing?"

"Not at all."

"Okay. What else?"

"Both Maxwell Novak and Carol Hester had reasons for wanting Aunt Liddy out of the way."

"You lost me. Why would Carol want her dead?"

"You didn't notice the way she stared at Jack?"

"So?"

The drinks arrived. The waitress managed to find a spot not covered by Post-its and deposited the glasses of tea along with a saucer of lemons. "Are you ready to order?"

"Two corned beef sandwiches and a cup of potato soup for each of us." Monah glanced at Casey to be sure she agreed.

"So," Casey said, pointing at her Post-it Notes after the waitress left, "I'm thinking office romance. Maybe Carol got jealous of Aunt Liddy's relationship with Jack. They were pretty close."

Monah's eyes widened, and she nodded. "Makes sense. But don't forget Jack."

"Excuse me?"

"You have to consider everyone, right?"

Casey agreed with a wave. "Well, yeah, but why would Jack kill her? They were friends."

Monah propped her elbows on the table and tapped her index fingers together. "Why, indeed."

Peeling the wrapper off her straw, Casey stuck it in her tea and took a sip. "Monah, you've lived here forever. What do you know about their relationship?"

"Jack and Lydia?"

"Uh-huh."

Monah squeezed a lemon slice into her tea, added a packet of Sweet'N Low, and stirred thoughtfully. "Gosh, they've been friends as long as I can remember. Even before John died."

"Who?"

"John. Jack's twin brother."

The tea in Casey's mouth nearly drowned her. She coughed it out, grabbed a napkin, and dabbed at her lips. Why hadn't Aunt Liddy ever told her this? "I didn't know Jack had a brother."

"Oh, yeah."

"What happened to him?"

"Well"—Monah's brow scrunched as she thought—"it was several years ago. Seems to me I remember my mom saying he was killed in a sailing accident or something."

"That's terrible!"

"It was sad, all right. Jack took it hard. He acted weird for a long time afterward, but Lydia took it even harder."

Casey cast her a blank look. "What?"

Disbelief clouded Monah's face. She pushed her glass aside and leaned over the table. "You knew Lydia and John were in love, right?"

Pain stabbed Casey's heart. Here was something else about Aunt Liddy she never knew. "No."

"Momma says that's why Lydia never married. She carried her love for John all these years."

Sympathy for Aunt Liddy's lost love clogged Casey's throat. She shook her head. "I didn't know. I wonder why Aunt Liddy never mentioned it."

"Maybe because it was so long ago?"

"Maybe." Casey picked up her fork and tapped the edge of her place mat. The table wobbled. Monah grabbed a couple of sweetener packets and shoved them under the leg.

The arrival of their sandwiches curtailed further conversation. Casey gathered up the Post-its and returned them to her purse before taking a bite of savory corned beef. "You're right. This stuff is delicious."

Monah wiped a dab of Thousand Island dressing from her mouth and nodded. "It's my favorite thing here."

Casey's thoughts filled the silence while they ate. Perhaps Aunt Liddy's love for John explained her close relationship with Jack. She could easily imagine her transferring some of that emotion to his look-alike. How tempted was she to fall into something deeper than friendship with Jack?

Most of Monah's sandwich had disappeared. "Tell me more about Carol," she said after a bit. "Do you have anything else to go on besides the way she was looking at Jack?"

Casey took a swallow from her glass. "Not really, but I will. I plan on questioning her tomorrow. After that, I'll take care of the gun business with. . .my father."

"You sure questioning Carol is a good idea? If your hunch is right, it could be dangerous. Shouldn't you tell the police and let them handle it?"

Adamant, Casey shook her head. "They think Aunt Liddy committed suicide. As far as they're concerned, this case is closed, whether they find her body or not. I'm not counting on any help from them."

"Well, you can count on me," Monah said as they pushed their plates aside. "Just tell me what you need me to do."

"Actually, there is something." Casey lifted an eyebrow. "You think you could ask your friend Brockman if the police have found out anything else about the person who stole Maxwell Novak's truck?"

"Sure." Monah grabbed the check before Casey could get to it. "It's on me. I invited you, remember?"

Casey smiled her thanks.

"What are you doing in the meantime?"

"I'm going to search the house to see if I can find that gun."

"Well, do you want me to help you do that first? I can talk to Mike anytime."

Casey glanced at her watch as they walked to the register. "No, I'd really like to know what they've uncovered."

Back at Aunt Liddy's house, Casey stepped out of the car and gave Monah a brisk wave. "Call me later?"

"You bet."

She watched her pull out of the driveway before going inside. At least now she had a plan of action. She took the stairs to her aunt's bedroom two at a time. It was the one place she could think of where Aunt Liddy might keep something of value. A thorough search of the closet revealed nothing but an old shoe box full of photos that fell on Casey's head as she rummaged through the top shelf.

"Yikes!" She jumped off the chair she'd been using as a ladder. Overhead, the string that turned on the closet light swung crazily. She grabbed it, stopped it from swinging, and rubbed at the bump on her head.

Photos lay everywhere. She started to scoop them into a pile, but one of Aunt Liddy as a young woman caught her eye. She was beautiful. Her long dark hair cascaded over her shoulders, and her eyes sparkled with life and happiness.

Casey dropped cross-legged onto the floor. So this was what love made a person look like? How sad to think that her beloved aunt had suffered so.

She lifted another picture. Aunt Liddy standing on a pier next to her boat. Aunt Liddy on her knees in the garden, blowing a kiss at someone. Aunt Liddy holding up the keys to her house. That one must have been taken shortly after she bought this place.

Deeper in the pile, Casey found a black-and-white picture of two boys in striped shirts. Each of them wore Converse tennis shoes and baseball caps with the Red Sox logo. They stood with their arms around the other's shoulders, and one of the boys pointed to the other's mouth, whose broad smile proudly displayed his missing teeth. Over his shoulder, the toothless boy balanced a baseball bat with a glove shoved on the end.

Twins. They looked to be about thirteen or fourteen years old.

Casey swallowed hard. Jack and John. One of them was the love Aunt Liddy lost as a girl. She drew in a sharp breath as she realized that most of the pictures were probably taken by the very same man.

"Oh, Aunt Liddy. I'm so sorry." She wiped a stray tear from her cheek.

A noise rose from the garden outside Aunt Liddy's window. She stood to look.

Fear leaped inside her chest. Once again, she managed to catch a brief glimpse of a shadowy figure running away from the house a second before the person disappeared into the woods.

Casey showered, dressed, and slipped into her shoes early the following Monday morning. There'd been no need for an alarm. She spent the night checking the windows for a shadowy figure that never reappeared. Without evidence, she couldn't go to Rafferty.

She hurried downstairs, fastening a silver hoop to her ear, anxious to get to Jack's office so she could question Carol Hester. Golden sunlight streamed through the kitchen window. She paused as she spied the rosebushes growing on one side of the garden. The wilted flowers were Aunt Liddy's favorite. Brown spots discolored the emerald leaves dotting the ground. She'd have to take a closer look when she got back.

Heeding the rumbling in her stomach, she toasted a slice of bread and held it between her teeth. With her purse slung over her shoulder, she backed out of the house, keys in hand.

The ornate offices of Kerrigan, Inc., weren't half as imposing as the receptionist who greeted her at the entrance. She sat behind a marbled counter, her sharp eyes taking Casey in at a glance. Red lips tight, she inclined her head to peer over her jeweled reading glasses.

"Can I help you?"

Casey flashed her most disarming smile. "Carol Hester, please."

"Your name?"

She hesitated. Lying didn't feel right, and she'd soon be in Carol's office anyway. "Casey Alexander."

"And the nature of your business?"

"I'm. . .just visiting."

Disapproval radiated from the receptionist's angular features. She blew a sigh through her narrow nose and picked up the phone. "Casey Alexander here to see you."

After a moment, she replaced the receiver and pointed down the carpeted hall. "Third door on your right, past the potted palms."

"She agreed to see me?"

The look the woman directed at her screamed "daft."

"Third door. Thanks." Casey beat a retreat.

Carol greeted her before she could knock, a question in her gaze. "Ms. Alexander? Please, come in." She whirled and strode back to the desk.

Unsure whether to close the door or leave it open, Casey compromised and left it half ajar. "I wanted to thank you—"

"Oh?" Carol sat in a high-backed leather office chair and motioned her to a seat. She shoved an open bag of M&M's into a drawer and crossed her arms. "For what?"

"For. . ." Casey eased into the chair. "Well, your presence at my aunt's memorial service, I guess."

Carol nodded after a moment. "Jack needed the support."

An opening! Casey leaned forward. "You and Jack must be pretty close for you to be so considerate of his feelings."

Her lips pursed. "I've worked for him for a long time."

"How long, exactly?"

Carol picked up the mechanical pencil lying next to her phone. She rolled it between thumb and index finger, a frown puckering the skin between her evenly arched brows. "Might I ask your purpose in coming to see me today, Ms. Alexander?"

Well, you see, Ms. Hester, I think you killed my Aunt Lydia, was probably not the best approach. Casey forced a smile. "I'm just trying to make sense of my aunt's death. I'm not convinced she committed suicide, but the only way to prove that is to meet with the people who knew her and see if anyone can give me a reason why someone would want to harm her."

Carol relaxed against the back of her chair. "And what have you found so far?"

"Well—"

The phone rang. Carol bid her pause with an upraised finger and answered it. "Kerrigan, Inc. Oh, good morning, Jack. No new messages. Yes, I put the file on your desk next to the bid we received from Red Stone Arsenal. Uh-huh. I will. Okay, thanks. See you soon."

Casey tore her gaze away from the picture on the wall of a young man holding a baseball bat. "That was Jack on the phone?"

Carol scribbled a message to herself on a worn steno pad. "Yes."

"He's not—" She pointed to the office adjoining Carol's.

"Jack went out of town on business. He should be back Friday. Where were we?"

Casey got up and walked over to the picture. Closer study revealed dimpled cheeks similar to Luke's and the words "Boston College" scrawled across the front of a vintage-style uniform. She glanced over her shoulder. "Is this Jack?"

Clearly exasperated, Carol gave a curt nod. "Yes."

"Does he still play?"

"He quit when his knees started giving him trouble."

"How long ago was that?"

"I don't know. . .fifteen, twenty years, maybe. What is this all about?" She rounded the desk and came to stand beside Casey, her arms crossed, a scowl on her face.

Casey took a deep breath and plunged in. "I wonder if you might tell me a little bit about your relationship to Jack. . .er. . .Mr. Kerrigan."

Her mouth dropped. "Excuse me?"

"I noticed you watching him at the memorial."

Carol straightened and pursed her thin lips even tighter. "He's my boss, Miss Alexander. Nothing more. Not like—"

Certain she knew what Carol had been about to say, Casey lifted her chin. "Go on."

"Jack was very close to your Aunt Lydia. I'm sure you realize the connection went much deeper than they let on."

"I was not aware of that, no."

"Well, it did, and I wasn't the only one who noticed."

"But you did notice?"

"So?"

"So I have to ask myself, Ms. Hester, if an employee as dedicated as you didn't resent the fact that another woman captured the attention of a boss you spent years trying to impress."

Carol's sharp intake of breath rasped through the silent office, and her polished nails pinched white half-moons in her plump forearms. "You think I killed Lydia because I'm in love with Jack?"

Undaunted by the hostility on Carol's face, Casey

leaned toward her. "Did you?"

"I am not a murderer, Ms. Alexander, and I resent the implication. I think it's time I asked you to leave." She stalked to the door and threw it open the rest of the way.

Casey stepped into the hallway just as the door crashed shut behind her. Down the hall, the receptionist stared, eyes wide and mouth agape.

For someone with nothing to hide, Carol Hester certainly was anxious to get rid of her. Tugging her cell phone from her purse, she flipped it open and dialed Monah's number. She answered just as Casey left Kerrigan, Inc., and crossed the parking lot toward her rental car.

"Hello?"

"It's me."

"Hi, Casey. Any luck?"

"Not much. How about you?"

"Same here. Mike said they're no closer to figuring out who took Maxwell's truck. There is one thing I found strange, though. No fingerprints. Anywhere. Almost like whoever took the truck knew what they were doing. I'm sorry, Casey. Looks like we've come to a dead end."

Casey sighed. "That's all right. Novak doesn't seem like the mastermind type anyway. Besides, Carol is a much more likely suspect."

Across the street, two customers exited Black's Floral, reminding her of the wilted flowers she'd spied from the kitchen window earlier. "Hey, Monah, I think there's something wrong with Aunt Liddy's roses, the ones she entered at the state fair last year. Do you think maybe Luke could take a look at them for me?"

"I'm sure he wouldn't mind. Why don't you give him a call?"

"I think I will. Thanks, Monah." She paused with her hand on the door handle. "See you tonight? I could really use. . .you know, when I'm looking through Aunt Liddy's things. . ."

"Don't worry. I'll help you find your dad's gun."

Her soft whisper eased Casey's anxiety. "Thanks, Monah. I'll see you then."

She hung up and slid the phone inside the pocket of her purse. Part of the day's difficulties were over, but the worst still lay ahead.

Luke followed Mrs. Teaser into her kitchen, listening to her chatter on about her irritating drippy faucet, all the while trying to keep from stepping on any paws or tails.

"Thank you so much for coming over, Luke. I don't get around like I used to, and having somebody handy to call on is such a blessing."

"No problem. That outfit looks nice on you."

She blushed with pleasure.

Cats lounged everywhere, on the floor, on the chairs around the table, even on the counter. Lionel, the cat who tried to eat everything in sight, sat in the corner of the room eyeing the bag Luke held, the end of his tail flicking.

He set his toolbox on the floor and turned to Mrs. Teaser. "You won't need to use the water here at the sink, will you?"

"I sure won't, Luke. You do whatever you need to do." She pulled out a chair, picked up the cat occupying it, and sat with the old feline in her arms. "I'll just stay here and keep you company."

"Great. I shouldn't be long."

"Take your time, dear. I've yet to find a good enough reason to rush through anything."

He smiled as he ducked under the sink to turn off the water valves. His dad often complained about how long Mrs. Teaser took to clean his house. He couldn't recall ever seeing her in a hurry.

A cat crawled into the cabinet with him and started purring. With the valve tightly in the OFF position, Luke started to pull himself out of the cabinet. As he passed the cat, it pressed its nose against his jaw and slid it all the way to his chin, purring the whole time, its tail straight in the air.

Ack. Did that cat just wipe its nose on me?

He stood, wiping his jaw with his sleeve while turning on the tap to run off all the water in the pipe. His cell phone rang just as he had to go back under the sink next to that cat to loosen the screws. *Saved.*

"Hello?" He leaned against the counter.

"Hey, Luke. It's Casey."

"Casey?" He spun around and peered out the window, his heart convulsing at the sound of her voice. "Something wrong?" Seemed as though there was always something happening to her. Why else would she call?

"Well, I'm not sure. I'm standing here at Aunt Liddy's favorite rosebushes, and they don't look too good."

He let out his breath in a rush. Something simple. "Describe them."

"They're all wilted."

"Did—"

"And don't ask if I tried watering them. I did. They still look sick."

He grinned at her defensive tone. "Okay, tell you what. I have to finish something first, but when I'm done, I'll head over there and take a look."

"Thanks, Luke. I hoped you'd say that."

Her soft voice warmed his heart. "I shouldn't be too long."

He flipped the phone closed, threw it on the counter, and went to work replacing the old faucet, more than ready to be away from the cats. Besides, Casey needed him.

What was it about cats' eyes that made them so intense and calculating? Or was he the only one who thought that way? Truth be told, he didn't really mind cats. It was just that Mrs. Teaser's seemed a little odd.

The old faucet was loose, so he stood and pulled it free, replacing it with the new one. A few minutes later, he turned on the water valves and checked for any leaks. So far, so good. He opened the tap for a moment then shut it off again.

"Is it working?"

"Yes, it"—a cat jumped up on the counter next to him—"seems to be fine." Lionel sat eyeing his cell phone, his tail still twitching. Luke snatched up the phone and tucked it in his pocket. Maybe the cat couldn't swallow it, but that didn't mean he wouldn't try.

The cat's body went rigid and tilted forward. He wasn't going to. . . Surely the cat wouldn't heave on him. Luke stepped away. Three heaves later, Lionel lurched and the offending item plopped into the sink. With a low growl, the freaky feline jumped to the floor and ran from the room.

What a disgusting cat. No wonder he was so skinny.

Luke hazarded a peek into the sink, his morbid curiosity forcing him to see what Lionel had found so appetizing. He leaned closer, not believing what he saw. Teeth? The cat swallowed teeth? He hadn't noticed any gaps in Mrs. Teaser's smile earlier.

"I don't know why he does that." She sighed. "What was it this time?"

"Ah—" He ran some water into the sink and washed the refuse down the drain, making certain the teeth didn't go with it. A small partial remained. He rinsed it clean and held it up for inspection.

"Have you lost a couple of teeth, Mrs. Teaser?"

"No." She stood next to him. "I haven't—" Her expression changed from interest to shock and then to something like fear. "Oh."

"Did they belong to Mr. Teaser?"

"No. Not exactly. I sort of found it." Guilt hung heavy on her face.

Luke stared at her. Okay, so the gossip about Mrs. Teaser's propensity to collect odd items might be true. Some even believed she squirreled away things from the houses she cleaned. But teeth?

"Found them where?"

She finally met his gaze. "Oh, Luke. I guess I need to confess."

"Confess what?" Or did he really want to know?

"Come," she said, motioning to the table, "sit down."

He sat next to her, the teeth still in his hand. She touched his arm.

"I found that in your dad's house. Years ago. Not long after your momma died."

"Dad's house? But Dad doesn't wear a partial."

"I know. Well, at least I was pretty sure he didn't. That's why I took it. I didn't figure he'd miss it. I thought maybe it belonged to one of his guests."

He tried to remember if any of his dad's friends wore anything like it. He handed it to her. "If no one has missed them after all these years, I doubt they'd want them now."

She pushed it back toward him. "You keep it. I shouldn't have taken it in the first place, and if you have it, Lionel won't try to eat it again."

But what was he going to do with it? "All right." He grabbed a napkin, wrapped the teeth in it, and stuffed it in his pocket as he stood. "I think you're all set, but if it starts dripping again, let me know." He grabbed his toolbox and the old faucet and headed for the door.

"Thank you, Luke. You're such a dear boy. No wonder Lydia thought so much of you."

The old familiar ache came back as he said his good-byes. He couldn't describe how much he missed her.

After stowing his toolbox, he jumped in his truck and headed out to meet Casey.

Luke found Casey sitting on the grass with the same dejected look as the rosebushes, what was left of the morning dew leaving damp spots on her jeans.

"Casey?"

She stroked one of the leaves between her fingers. More of them lay on the ground under the bushes. "Her favorite roses." She met his gaze, her eyes red-rimmed. "Was there something I was supposed to do to keep them alive? Did I do something wrong?"

He knelt at her feet, identifying with her desire to hang on to anything of Lydia's. "Nothing needed to be done. This isn't your fault."

She rubbed the sleeve of her sporty denim shirt across her cheek, still sniffling. "Well, do you think you can save them?"

The hopeful expression on her face made him want to say yes, but from what he could see, the bushes were beyond help. But why? There was no fungus he could see, no beetles on the ground. "I don't know yet. Let me check a few things first."

The leaves from tip to base hung like icicles losing their grip to the first day of spring. Their color had faded from brilliant green to the sickly shade of canned spinach. No disease would kill a plant this fast. But then, he hadn't really paid attention to Lydia's garden. The bushes could have been dying for a while now.

He scooped up a handful of dirt from under the bush and sniffed. It didn't have the rich loamy scent he expected. This stuff smelled acidic.

Casey scooted up beside him. "Why are you frowning? What's wrong?"

He blew out a long stream of air and pushed the cap back on his head. "They can't be saved, Casey. Either they've been sprayed with something, or something's wrong with the soil."

"Like what?"

He tossed the dirt back under the bush and brushed his hands against his jeans. "I'm not sure. I could have it tested, but it still won't save the roses."

Her shoulders slumped. "So now what?"

He wanted nothing more than to be able to give her some good news. It seemed she'd had nothing but problems since she'd arrived.

"Would it help if I offered to replace them? I could dig these up and have some new ones in before dark."

Hope flared in her eyes for just a moment, replaced once more by gloom. "If there's something wrong with the soil, won't the new ones just die anyway?"

"Not if I dig all the old dirt out, like a six by four foot hole, and refill it with some from my place."

She peered up into his face, her eyes piercing his. "You'd do that?"

In a heartbeat. "Consider it done."

He stood and held out his hand to help her up. "You get Lydia's wheelbarrow, and I'll get my shovel."

Minutes later, he drove the shovel deep. Scoop by scoop, he dug until the wheelbarrow was loaded. After dumping it at the edge of Lydia's property, he repeated the process.

Casey stepped next to the hole. "Need some help?"

Her gaze traveled over his chest, lingered at his mouth,

and swung to his face. Pink filled her cheeks as she met his eyes. The knowledge that he affected her sent a bolt of pleasure straight into his heart. He gave her a knowing grin as he handed her a pair of gloves, allowing his touch to linger.

"Sure. See if that bush is loosened enough to pull out." He did the same to the ones near him. All of them came out with a quick tug. The roots were a darker color than normal. He dropped one in the back of his truck, covered it with a burlap bag, and went back to finish.

Casey looked up from the hole. "Is that deep enough?"

"Nope. I want it deep and wide enough to make sure nothing will affect the new plants." He dug the shovel in again.

"I can help with the digging, you know. I'm stronger than I look."

He reached over and squeezed her bicep, all the while fighting a grin. "Hmmm. Make a muscle."

She smiled and took a playful swat at him. He ducked out of the way with a laugh then handed the shovel to her.

"I'll get another one."

Back in moments, he jumped into the hole and set to work opposite her, trying to watch without being obvious. She struggled with the shovel, her foot slipping off the blade time after time. After a few minutes, there was no doubt she wasn't used to this type of labor. Maybe getting her to talk would allow her to slow down and rest. "Would a Web site do my business much good? Would it be worth the expense and pay off my investment in the long run?"

As though he'd flipped a switch, he could almost see a jolt of energy jerk through Casey's mind and move her into high speed.

"Oh, I can see great potential, Luke. We could have a seedling grow into a beautiful flowering bush or a rosebud open into full bloom right before the viewers' eyes as they look over your home page. There could also be a page for answering questions, like an 'Ask the Gardener' section or something. And we could upgrade to selling seeds and bulbs instead of just plants."

Her enthusiasm made it obvious she loved her work. And Luke enjoyed hearing her say "we." A site would be worth the investment just for the time they'd spend building it together.

"So what do you think?"

"Huh?"

She crouched inside the hole and stared up at him while she scooped at the soil with her hands. "Did you even hear anything I said?"

"Of course. All great ideas." *I'm sure.* A picture of her with the dirt smudges on her face would look good on the site, too.

She stopped her digging. "I'm wondering, Luke. Are you sure you can afford a site?"

He sat, his legs dangling over the edge of the hole. "What makes you ask that? Do I act or look as though my business is in trouble?"

"No. It's just. . ."

"Just what?"

She focused her attention on the dirt dribbling through her fingers. "Well, I heard you were denied a loan."

The memory of seeing her and Monah in the bank that day with the loan officer came back to him. "Oh. And so you naturally assumed I was in a bind."

She shrugged.

He bumped his hat back with his thumb and looked her in the eyes. "Well, just so you know, I'm not in financial trouble. I wanted a loan to build an extension on my nursery. It'll just have to wait till next year."

"Oh. I'm sorry." Her soft voice sounded tender, genuine. Best of all, she didn't shrink away, and if he moved just a couple of inches closer. . .

He removed his hand. "No problem. You can ask me anything. I've got nothing to hide."

Something white dropped from her fingers as she sifted through the soil. She scooped it up again and held a small bone gingerly between finger and thumb, a look of disgust on her face.

"Don't tell me—you buried a cat here, too."

He jumped into the hole. "You saw that the other day, huh?"

She smiled and handed the bone to him. "How many cats has Mrs. Teaser asked you to bury, anyway?"

"I never buried a cat here. Lydia always took care of these roses." He took the bone from her and examined it. "Looks pretty old. And as deep as this hole is, it could have been here for centuries." He stood and threw it into the wheelbarrow.

"Here's another one." Casey tossed a larger bone at his feet and continued digging through the soil. "And another." She stood and took two steps back, bumping into him. "I don't want to dig there anymore. That's gross."

He smiled and helped her from the hole. "I'll finish. It'll only take a few more scoops anyway."

When he scraped his spade over the area Casey had just vacated, more small bones appeared.

Okay, that's weird.

He dug faster. With gentle thrusts, he elongated the hole by several inches. He stopped when the shovel hit something hard. He knelt once more and started brushing at the dirt with his hand. The sight of a jaw with teeth still intact stopped his heart. Casey's scream slammed it back into action.

13

Casey paced the length of the porch, sweat running down her back. A few feet away, police cars cluttered the driveway like cumbersome pandas with flashing red hats. Finally, Luke appeared, Detective Rafferty at his side.

She clasped her hands tight. "Well?"

Luke leaped up the bottom stair and slid his arm around her shoulders. "They're gonna send the bones to Boston for analysis. Rafferty says it'll be a week, maybe more."

"Unless we can get a dental on the victim, which I doubt, since some of the teeth are missing." Rafferty gestured to Officer Brockman, who, along with several uniformed officers, was picking through the pile of dirt Luke had dumped at the edge of the property. "They're probably in there. We'll be lucky to find anything, what with the mess you two made."

Casey shoved her hands to her hips. "We thought we were digging up roses, not excavating a crime scene."

"Yeah, well, intentional or not, you two just made our job a lot harder."

Casey bit her tongue to keep from yelling. Rafferty was only doing his job, albeit not very well. She nodded, and he left to rejoin the officers in the garden.

"How ya doin'?"

She looked up. Luke still held her. Savoring the sense of security his touch provided, she wanted to pretend infirmity, maybe even faint and fall into his arms. He grinned at the same moment as she and dropped his arm.

"I'll take that as an okay."

A large utility truck rumbled to a stop in the road and backed up the driveway, the caution horn beeping.

"What's that?"

"A generator." Luke pointed to the garden. "Looks like they plan on being here awhile. You want to go get something to eat?"

"Can we?" Casey glanced uncertainly at Detective Rafferty's rigid back. Encased in a coarse wool blazer, he was pricklier than a sandbur and a lot less welcome.

"I think he's already asked all the questions he's going to, but I'll double check."

He returned a few moments later, his keys dangling from his fingers. "All set." After settling her in the passenger side of his Chevy, Luke rounded the driver's side and drove the short distance to Fred's Diner. Among the many patrons, Monah sat by herself at one of the checkered-cloth-covered booths.

"Mind if we join you?" Casey said, loving the feel of Luke's hand on her back as he escorted her inside.

Monah's smile stretched from ear to ear. "Hey, guys. You two on a date?"

Casey slid into the seat opposite her, and Luke followed, his knee bumping hers as he sat. She hid a smile. *I wish.* "Not hardly. We just came from the house. The police are there. You'll never guess what we found in Aunt Liddy's garden."

A greasy french fry dropped from Monah's fingers. She grabbed a napkin to rub the oil off and leaned over the table. "What?"

"Bones. Human ones," Luke said. "And they look to

be several years old."

"Bones!" Monah ducked her head when a few of the customers glanced their way. "Whose?"

"No idea," Casey said, lowering her voice to match Monah's. "Detective Rafferty said it would take at least a week to get the forensics report back from Boston."

Over Monah's shoulder, Casey saw Carol Hester bolt from a booth near the window. She neither looked at them nor acknowledged their presence as she strode to the cash register.

Casey tapped Monah's hand and inclined her head toward the door. "How long has she been here?"

"She came in after I did."

"Do you think she heard us?"

Almost on cue, Carol swung to glare at them, her face red and eyes hard.

"Hey, Carol. How's it going?" Luke propped his arm across the back of the seat, looking for all the world as though he talked about human corpses every day.

Relieved by his quick intervention, Casey pasted on a smile and met Carol's gaze.

Carol dismissed him with a wave and focused her laser stare on Casey. "Did I hear you say you found bones at your aunt's place?"

By now, the private conversations going on in the diner had ceased. Ten or more pairs of eyeballs bounced back and forth from Carol to Casey.

"Um. . .yeah. Sort of. We're not really sure what we found."

"When will you know?"

Monah cleared her throat. "You know what? I forgot I told my assistant, Miss Magrew, that I'd be back from lunch early today to help her restock overdue library books. Casey, did you still want to check out that guide you asked me about?"

"Huh?" Luke and Casey asked in unison.

"You know, that one on defensive driving." Monah's bulging eyes were almost comical as she tilted her head and wagged her brows at Carol.

"Oh, that one. Yeah, she still needs it," Luke said. Casey poked him in the ribs.

Monah dropped ten dollars on the table next to her bill, and all three of them hurried out the door. A few seconds later, Carol stepped out onto the sidewalk, her neck craned as she watched them scurry away.

"What was that all about?" Luke asked, tossing a glance over his shoulder at Carol.

"You thinking what I'm thinking?" Casey said to Monah, linking her arm through Luke's and pulling him along.

"What? What are you two thinking?"

Monah shoved open the library door, and all three almost fell inside. "We're thinking," she said between gasps, "that's it's time we stepped up the investigation into Carol Hester."

14

The glow of the computer screen cast a weak circle of light around the library. Casey sighed and rubbed her eyes. Hard to believe they'd been researching Carol's name for almost three hours. "Anything?" Luke's voice rumbled through the rows of books.

She glanced at him. Since the library boasted only one computer, he'd resorted to using the microfiche. Next to him, Monah sorted through old newspapers.

"Not yet," Casey said. The muscles in her neck and shoulders burned. She sat back and tried to massage away the stiffness.

Luke rose and stood behind her. "Here, let me do that." He pushed her hands aside. Within moments his strong fingers worked much of the tension from her shoulders. "All right, let me in there." He patted her arm.

She scooted out of the chair. "What can I do?"

"Take a break. Both of you." He glanced at Monah, whose ink-smudged face made her look like a raccoon caught rummaging through the trash.

"Me, too?"

He jerked his keys from the pocket of his jeans. "Yep. Come back in an hour. Bring food."

"No argument here. I'm starved," she said. "But don't tell anyone we ate in here. You could cause me a great deal of trouble."

"Yeah, okay. I could use a break." Casey stretched from side to side, easing the ache in her lower back. "Got a preference?"

"Pizza," he and Monah said in unison.

She laughed. "Pizza it is." The keys jangled as Luke tossed them to her. "Ready, Monah?"

Together, they exited the library and made for the pizza place on the edge of town. Once they ordered, they claimed a booth near the door and sat down to wait.

"Here." Monah slid a cola across the table to her. "The food's gonna be at least twenty minutes. Are you thirsty?"

"Yes." Dust from the library made Casey's throat drier than the papers Monah had been flipping through. She grabbed the cold soda can, popped the top, and took a long drink. She looked around the tiny restaurant.

"This is a cute place. Has it been here long?"

Monah nodded. "A little while. It's takeout mostly, but they did add on last year so they could put in a couple of tables."

"Must've been a good investment." Casey motioned to the crowd of people seated across the room from them.

Jukebox music drifted from the corner. Green gingham curtains livened the windows. The scent of fresh dough wafted from the kitchen. A nice family place, Casey decided.

"Yeah. Pine Mills needed a good place to eat. Used to be, we had to go to into Worcester or Marlborough. Now we've got three restaurants. We're growing." She grinned, and her dark eyebrows rose behind the glasses.

Casey laughed. "Right. Booming." She fixed Monah with a curious stare. "So why do you stay?"

"Huh?"

"Pine Mills. What keeps you here?"

Monah ran the tip of her finger around the rim of her can. "Besides the bustle and excitement?"

Casey didn't answer Monah's smile. For the first time, she sensed something deeper in her friend, something she hadn't seen before.

"My parents are getting older." Monah looked away, a troubled frown wrinkling her brow. "I want to be here for them, like they were for me."

"You mean growing up?"

"I mean. . ." She wadded up the paper from her straw and dropped it in the ashtray. "Did you know I was adopted?"

A country song wailed in the background as Casey hesitated. "No one ever mentioned it."

"I was four. My mother was more interested in doing drugs than raising a child. I never knew my father."

"I'm sorry." Identifying with the pain of not knowing her father left a dull ache in Casey's chest.

Monah shrugged. "Thanks. It was hard at first. I spent a couple of years in foster care moving from family to family before the Trenarys adopted me. It took me awhile to get settled, really feel like I belonged, but their steadfast love helped me through. That, and discovering that I have a heavenly Father who'll never leave me."

Casey couldn't quite meet Monah's earnest stare or the question that lurked there. She plucked at the tab on her soda can. "How do you do it? How do you keep trusting God when you've been through so much? Aren't you angry?"

"What have I got to be angry about? My whole life has been one miracle after another." She laid her hand on Casey's forearm. "God loved me so much that He personally walked with me through each and every day. That was before I even knew He existed. What child could ask for a more loving parent? Why won't you believe that God cares for you that much?"

Maybe because the example of her earthly father had left her gun-shy? Richard's face popped unbidden into Casey's mind. He claimed he wanted to talk, maybe reconcile some of their differences, yet she resisted. But what if he really did want to work things out? Did she dare trust him after all he'd put their family through? And if he did mean all he said, if she let go of all the hurt and bitterness and accepted him, then what?

"Pizza for Trenary."

Casey looked up, relieved when the girl behind the counter signaled their food was ready. She and Monah scooted from the booth, paid the bill, and rode back to the library, only stopping long enough to pick up a two-liter bottle of cola.

Luke leaned back and rubbed his stomach when they entered. "Hope you girls brought plenty. I'm starved."

Monah laughed. "Are you kidding? Between the two of us, we could finish off this pizza by ourselves. Casey'll just have to settle for the breadsticks."

Casey laughed and snatched a thick slice out of the box, and the three of them sat at one of the tables to eat.

"So, any luck?" Monah asked as they munched.

"Just so many rabbit trails. I hate research. I couldn't stand doing it in high school, and this feels just like I'm back in Miss Tait's English class."

"Ugh." Monah rolled her eyes. "Don't remind me."

Casey's gaze switched from one to the other. "Who's Miss Tait?"

"Honors English." Cheese dripped from Luke's pizza. He stuck it back on top and took a bite, then swallowed. "She hated me."

Monah screwed the top off the two-liter. She grabbed mugs from her office, poured drinks, and handed one to him. "Don't spill that. I'm in trouble if anybody figures out we ate in here. Anyway, unless you were Milton Bradley, Miss Tait hated everyone. Remember him? Teacher's pet if ever I saw one. What happened to him?"

"He left town about six or seven years ago. He's a lawyer now. I think I heard he changed his name. Who wouldn't, with a name like that? We used to tease him—"

Casey set her cup down with a thud. "What did you say?"

"Huh?" Luke paused with his pizza midair.

"He changed his name?"

"Yeah. Why?"

Casey shook her head in disbelief. "Good grief. All this time we've been looking for someone named Carol Hester. But what if she changed her name? What if she were someone else?"

Monah and Luke exchanged a glance. He set down his food and grabbed a napkin to rub the grease from his fingers. "How would we know? Who could we ask?"

"I know someone." Monah tugged her cell phone from her purse. "And I'll bet she's home."

Moments later, Monah's mother confirmed what Casey suspected. Carol had moved to Pine Mills over twenty years ago, with no past and no friends. The only thing that gave any indication as to where she'd come from had been the Boston Red Sox bumper sticker on her beat-up Honda Civic. That, and the gossip Monah's mom said circulated when she arrived, rumors of a shady past and criminal record.

"So how do we track her down?" Luke followed Casey

to the computer and peered over her shoulder as she typed.

On the other side, Monah hovered with the cell phone still pressed to her ear. "Let's drop her name, move our search back twenty years, and narrow it to crimes in the Boston newspapers."

"A hundred and twenty thousand results!" Luke groaned. "We'll never get through all of those."

"Hold on." Casey's fingers flew over the keyboard. On a hunch, she added "Carol" and "arrested" to the keywords and hit SEARCH. This time, only a handful of articles with the name *Carol* in the text popped up.

"Wait!" Monah covered Casey's hand before she could click on the first link. Eyes closed, her lips moved in silent prayer. "Okay. Now."

All three inhaled deeply as Casey moved the mouse. Within moments, a much younger version of Carol Hester stared back at them from the screen. Luke's low whistle echoed through the darkened library.

"Carol Jenks," Casey whispered. "She used to be Carol Jenks."

Monah bent closer. "Why didn't she change her first name?"

"Nostalgia? Maybe she couldn't ditch her old life completely."

Luke grunted. "What'd she do?"

" 'Boston Woman Arrested on Charges of Embezzlement,' " Casey read. "It says here she worked for a shipping company in their accounts payable department and started tampering with the books."

The room fell silent as all three skimmed through the story. One by one, they finished and drew back.

"That's it. That's the connection." Goose bumps pricked Casey's flesh. "Carol must be up to her old tricks."

Monah snapped her fingers. "She works for Jack. You think she started stealing money from him?"

Luke drew a sharp breath and spun his back to them. Casey shot Monah a quick glance, but she looked as dumbfounded as Casey felt. She went to him and placed her hand on his tense shoulder. "What is it?"

Luke turned, his brows drawn in a frown. "The other day, I had lunch with Carol. She spilled a drink in my lap."

"I remember." Casey nodded. "It was the same day I found Aunt Liddy's shoe."

"Right."

"So?"

He hesitated, indecision warring with suspicion in his eyes. "She had an envelope stuffed with money in her purse. She told me it was the bank deposit."

Monah gave a low whistle. "So that's it, then. She really is stealing money."

Casey paced the length of the counter. "Aunt Liddy must've found out about it, so Carol did her in and then made it look like suicide."

"Okay, slow down. The article said she was arrested, not convicted," Luke warned, but Casey plunged ahead.

"All we have to do is figure out how she did it." Her head snapped up. "A stakeout. We'll take turns following her around town—"

"—and keep watch on her activities." Monah sounded as breathless as Casey felt.

"Write down any odd or unusual visits—"

"Ladies."

Casey whirled to face Monah. "Do you think you can get an address for me? We definitely want to watch her house."

"No problem. Maybe I should go first. I don't work tomorrow."

"And I should question her again. If I stop by the office, I might even get a glimpse of her files."

"Ladies!"

Both Casey and Monah turned to stare at Luke.

"This is interesting, I admit, but don't you think you're jumping to an awful lot of conclusions based on one envelope and a mistake Carol made over twenty years ago?"

Little by little, Casey's racing heart slowed. She crossed her arms, fists clenched. "So what do you suggest?"

His gaze softened, and he gently pried her hands open to be held in his warm ones. "Sleep on it, Casey. Let things stew awhile, maybe even pray for wisdom. It can't hurt, and it may spare Carol some heartache if you're wrong."

Monah's sigh rustled like a gentle breeze. "He's right. We should wait, till morning at least."

Both of their faces bore the same look of concern. Casey hated to agree, even though she knew they were right. Finally, she nodded. "Okay, but I still think she's the one."

"She may be." He rubbed her arm and led her toward the door. "But if so, then our best bet is to proceed with caution. Monah, do you need any help locking up?"

Monah shook her head. Luke and Casey stepped out onto the sidewalk, dimly lit by the old-fashioned lanterns that lined Main Street.

"Thanks, Luke. I appreciate your help today. I know you're probably right about taking this thing slowly. I wouldn't want to scare Carol into hiding. Brandy Purcell always conducts her investigations one step at a time."

He moved closer, shielding her from the nip in the night air with the warmth of his body. "Who's Brandy Purcell?"

"She's. . ." With him so close, she couldn't think straight. "Oh, never mind."

"Good. I'm more interested in you anyway."

"You are?"

"Uh-huh." He smiled. "You look cute today. There ought to be a law against those jeans you have on."

She glanced down at her clothes, still grimy from when they'd been digging earlier. "You gotta be kidding."

Suddenly, she knew he wasn't. His face grew serious, and his gaze moved to her mouth.

"Luke?"

He leaned toward her. "Yeah?"

"If you want to kiss me. . ."

She couldn't bring herself to say more. He cupped her chin with one hand and pulled her close with the other, lingering, his breath mingling with hers for a fraction of a second. His hold on her tightened, and then his mouth claimed hers.

Luke's kiss blew over her like a late summer storm. She felt it from the top of her head to the soles of her feet. Gentle, sweet, it was everything she'd hoped it would be, except that it ended too soon.

"Oops. Guess I should have waited a moment before I came out."

Luke took a shuddering breath and smiled at Monah as he pulled away. "Actually, I think you made it just in time."

Casey couldn't agree more. It would have been easy to be swept away by such powerful emotions as the ones Luke stirred. She lifted her hand to smooth her hair, but changed her mind and shoved it into her pocket when she saw her fingers shake. "No problem, Monah. You ready to go?"

"Yep." Monah pointed away from town. "I'm walking home, so you two can go on ahead if you want."

Indecision tore at Luke's features. He glanced down the street in the direction of Monah's house and back at Casey. "I don't like the idea of her walking by herself after dark. . . ."

Joy bubbled up from Casey's middle. It was enough that she knew he wanted to be alone with her. She grabbed Monah's hand. "It's late, and there's a murderer on the loose. We'll take you."

Though short, the ride to Monah's house helped cool the fire Luke had ignited in Casey's veins. She caught a glimpse of Monah's quick thumbs-up as they dropped her off and backed out of the driveway. Neither one mentioned the kiss as they rode out of town. Nor did they speak until they hit the driveway leading to Aunt Liddy's house.

The lights from the utility truck shone like a beacon from the backyard. A crew from the gas company joined the police officers scrambling through the dirt. They'd probably had to turn off the gas during the excavation.

Casey bit her lip and fumbled for the catch on her seat belt. "They're still at it."

"Yeah." Luke slowed and came to a stop. "Are you going to be all right? I can take you back to town if you want. There's a bed-and-breakfast not far from Monah's house."

"No thanks." She reached for the handle, but Luke caught her hand.

"Wait." He climbed from the truck, circled around, and opened the door for her. He led her up the steps to the front porch. "I'll call you in the morning, then?"

Casey fidgeted with her keys. Saying good night to him was much harder than she'd expected. "You'd better. Otherwise, I'll be hunting Carol down without you."

He smiled. "Wouldn't want that." His warm fingers closed over hers as he took the keys and unlocked the house. "Good night, Casey."

She hesitated. With so many interested onlookers watching them, she knew he wouldn't kiss her again. Still. . .

He laid the keys in her palm, holding her hand a fraction longer than necessary, his warm gaze telling her everything his lips didn't. And when he stepped away to close the door, Casey felt as though she had been kissed, and she never wanted it to end.

15

R elax. He'll be here soon." Monah's voice cut through
Casey's thoughts like viruses in a software program.

She left the parlor window with a sigh. Monah was
right. She'd been watching the clock on the mantel for
over an hour, even though Richard had told her in his
phone message that he wouldn't arrive until eleven. It was
only ten thirty. It didn't help that his visit forced her and
Luke to hold off their investigation of Carol until the
afternoon.

Her hands felt damp, jittery. Better skip that fourth
cup of coffee. She joined Monah on the couch. "I wish
he'd hurry up so we can get this over with. Maybe I should
keep looking without him."

Monah shrugged. "We already searched the downstairs
and bedrooms. What's left?"

"The attic." Casey rose and went to stand by the
banister. "Call me when he gets here?"

"You got it."

She climbed the stairs, feet dragging. Going through
Aunt Liddy's things felt like such an invasion. Thankfully,
Monah arrived early, or she'd never have been able to get
started.

A blast of stale air struck her as she shoved open the
heavy attic door. They'd be in for a miserable time if they
had to search long. The unusually warm day would only
get hotter. Good thing she'd dressed in a simple short-
sleeved top. She'd probably wish for shorts soon.

A single bulb shed dim light as she flipped the switch

next to the door. The small window on the far end of the attic did little to dispel the gloom. She pressed forward, her blue flip-flops slapping against her heels. Already, her hair clung to her damp shoulders. She twisted it into a ponytail then reached for the first box.

Pantsuits. Dresses. The thick layer of dust that covered the top of the carton attested to their age. Casey shoved it under the rafters next to a rickety bicycle. Within minutes, three more boxes joined the first, all of them filled with old clothing and smelling of mothballs.

"How ya doin' up there?"

She poked her head out from behind an antique trunk and hollered toward the stairs. "Fine. Is he here?"

"Not yet. Do you want me to come up there and help you look?"

"Nah. I don't think we'll be able to hear the doorbell if we're both up here. I could use an ice water though. This place is a steam bath."

"Coming right up."

She sorted through a chest of homemade Christmas decorations while she waited for Monah to appear, many of them marked with both Richard and Lydia's names. She fought the hurt roiling in her stomach. Why wouldn't Aunt Liddy have kept the things Richard made? He was her brother, after all.

To Liddy, from Richard. Merry Christmas.

She dropped the magnetic picture frame with a photo of the two of them standing in front of a tree back into the box. She didn't even own a picture of her father. He hadn't been around long enough.

"Here you go, sweetie." Monah handed her a glass wet with condensation.

"Thanks. I didn't realize it would be so warm up here." Casey took a long drink, letting the cold water soothe her tight throat.

"Lydia sure had a lot of stuff. Didn't she throw anything away?"

Casey gestured around the room. "She was the world's worst packrat. Although I do think these"—she held up a pair of bell-bottomed blue jeans, bright with painted flowers—"are making a comeback."

Monah laughed and snatched the pants from Casey's grasp. "Lydia wore bell-bottoms? What do you think?" She held them up to her waist and struck a pose.

"I think they were ugly the first time around."

Their moment of laughter was interrupted by a voice from downstairs.

"Anyone home?"

Leave it to Richard to catch them unawares.

"In the attic." Casey's heart pounded with every fall of his feet on the stairs. She reached up and smoothed her ponytail.

Soon his figure emerged in the doorway. "I rang the bell. Guess you couldn't hear me."

Casey stood, discomfited by his presence, even more by his crisp attire. Compared to the neat polo shirt and wrinkle-free slacks he wore, her clothes looked downright shabby. *Give him a minute. He'll be sweating bullets in no time. Then we'll see how good he looks.* She snorted and coughed to cover it up. "Dust."

"Yeah, dust." Monah waved her hand as though to brush it away. "Um. . .sorry, Mr. Alexander. We didn't hear you come in."

"No problem. And please, call me Richard."

"Okay, Richard," Casey said before Monah could reply. She felt a stab of remorse at the stricken look Monah directed at her for her tone. Now was not the time for barbed comebacks. They would only make Monah uncomfortable. She determined to be nice.

"We've already spent a couple of hours looking. So far, no luck, but we only just tackled the attic. I'm sure the gun Aunt Liddy left you is here somewhere. If you'd like to help, you can start by searching over there." She pointed to a dresser resting in the far corner of the room. "Monah and I will finish up here."

"I'll do whatever you want me to do, Casey, though I'm sure you realize it's not the gun I'm concerned about."

"Okay, you know what—" She took a deep breath and started again. "I heard what you said at the memorial service about finding a way to reconcile and all that. Maybe you meant it, maybe not. Right now, dealing with Aunt Liddy's death is all I can handle. Please try to respect that." Angered by the tears she felt threatening, Casey balled her fists and took a step back.

Her breathing sounded loud in the sudden silence. Richard's gaze fell as he nodded and trudged toward the dresser.

Did he have to act so sincere? Casey stifled a growl and shoved a box aside with her foot, ignoring the sad look on Monah's face as she brushed past and headed for an armoire stuffed with quilts. Thanks to Richard, she'd spent many nights crying herself to sleep as a child. Did he really expect her to forget all that just because he apologized? And what about Mom? His intentions did her no good now that she was gone.

She jerked a blanket from the stack and regretted the

move when a cloud of dust enveloped her head.

"Easy there, killer," Monah whispered. "Your allergies are gonna go haywire if you're not careful."

Casey plunked the quilt onto the floor. "Who said I have allergies?" She promptly sneezed.

Monah grinned.

"You're going to get on my last nerve," Casey said, drawing her arm across her burning eyes.

Monah's smile broadened. "Too late. I think he already did that." She pointed toward Richard and then ducked to avoid the feather pillow Casey tossed at her head.

Casey reached for a second pillow, but her fingernails scraped a wooden chest instead. She bent to examine it.

"What's that?"

"I don't know."

Secured by thick leather straps, the small chest hunkered at the bottom of the armoire. Casey tugged it from its hiding place. It landed with a thud on the floor.

"Find something?" Richard strode toward them, curiosity evident on his face.

"Maybe. It looks like one of those old trunks people used to use for luggage. It's not real big though."

Monah jerked up on the handle. "And it's locked. Anybody got a key?"

Casey snapped her fingers. "Aunt Liddy sent me a key just before she passed away. Do you think—?"

"Go get it." Monah shoved her arm.

Casey hurried down the stairs, found her purse on the table next to the couch, and rummaged through the contents until her fingers closed around the small key box.

"Got it," she said, huffing as she bolted back into the attic.

Both Richard and Monah hunched over her shoulder as she fumbled with the lock. It refused to budge.

"Spit on it."

"What?" Casey stared at Monah.

"I read it in a book once. Try it."

"Couldn't hurt," Richard added.

"Fine." Casey pooled a bit of saliva in her mouth and then let it drip in one long icky string.

"Eww," Monah groaned.

"Well!" Casey dried her lips with the back of her hand. "I don't know how to spit. That's a guy thing."

Richard grimaced. "Not every guy."

"Whatever." Monah waved. "Try the key again."

She inserted it into the lock. This time, with a little bit of finagling, it opened.

"What is it?"

"What's in there?"

Casey lifted a bundle of letters tied with ribbon. "Looks like just some old memoirs."

"No, there's something else." Monah pointed to a leather case at the bottom of the chest. She pulled it out and handed it to Richard. "The gun?"

He flipped open the top to reveal a pearl-handled Colt pistol, the barrel tarnished with age.

Casey brushed hair from her face. "At least that's done." A look of pain flashed across Richard's features, one that gave her pause. Could it be he meant everything he'd said? "I mean—"

"Hey, what's this?" Monah lifted a small pouch, held closed with a leather drawstring.

Casey exchanged the stack of letters with her for the pouch. "There's something inside."

She worked the knot on the drawstring until it came loose. The contents of the pouch tumbled out onto her palm—three stones, similar in size and appearance to the one she'd lost at the park.

"What are they?" Monah asked, picking one of them up and holding it toward the light.

"I've no idea. It's just like the one I found in Aunt Liddy's shoe."

Richard drew in a sharp breath. "You've seen these before?"

"Yeah. Do you know what they are?"

"Can I see it?" His fingers brushed her palm as he took the stone and brought it up for a closer look. "Doesn't look like anything special. Maybe she bought them as souvenirs from a trip or something." He dropped the rock back into her hand.

"I don't think so. They're too unusual. Don't you think so, Monah?"

"Yeah. And why would she have stuck them in the attic if they were a souvenir?"

He shrugged. "Everybody's got junk they don't have room for. Lydia was the worst about keeping stuff around."

Casey shook her head. "But she put them in this box and mailed me the key. That doesn't seem strange to you? Like maybe she wanted me to find the rocks? They must have special significance for her to have gone to such effort."

"And don't forget the one in her shoe. If you ask me, Lydia was leaving a trail of bread crumbs," Monah added.

Richard stumbled upright and tossed a hurried glance at his watch. "Um. . .I forgot I wanted to get to the bank before it closes. Can't leave this thing just lying around, right?" The gun case nearly slipped from his grasp as he waved it around. "Figured I'd have them hold it for me in a safety deposit box until I can find a more permanent place to live."

"Richard, wait. These stones—"

"I'm sorry, Casey. I'd really better get going. Thanks for taking the time to do this, though. I know. . .it was hard for you." He jerked toward the door and disappeared down the stairs.

Casey's mouth hung agape. He looked downright jittery. "What was that?"

Monah dropped the rock back into Casey's palm. "No idea, but I think you'd better find out what those things are, pronto."

"How? Research it at the library?"

Monah rose. "Lydia ordered a book about rocks, or stones, or something like that through the interlibrary loan. It came in just after she died. I forgot all about it."

"We should go get it." Casey bolted upright. "I'm sure Aunt Liddy's death is tied to these things somehow."

"Okay. What about these?" The letters slipped from the ribbon that bound them as she held them up for Casey to see. "Oh no!" She fumbled, too late, to catch them. They scattered across the floor. "Sorry, Casey."

"No problem. Let's just pick them up. . ." Casey paused with her hand on one of the letters. A name jumped out at her from the front of the envelope. She looked at Monah, dumbfounded. "These are from John Kerrigan."

"What?"

"Look." She turned the envelope so Monah could see it. Monah took the letter then bent to retrieve more. "So is this one. And this one."

A tattered divan rested near the window. Casey sank onto it, letters in her lap.

"Whoa. You all right?"

She nodded. "Do me a favor? Pick up the book and bring it back here. Something tells me I need to see what's in these letters."

"Are you sure? Why don't you read them downstairs? It's cooler."

"I'll be fine." She looked up, worried. "Just hurry back, okay?"

To her relief, Monah nodded and scurried out of the attic, leaving Casey alone, a handful of Aunt Liddy's past clutched in her cold fingers.

16

Luke hobbled to his truck nursing his left thumb. Preoccupation. If it wasn't the number one cause of accidents, it had to be on the list of the top five.

The job of landscaping Mrs. Dolan's yard this morning couldn't have gotten over soon enough. Between thoughts of Casey and the kiss they shared, and Carol's past, possibly current, crime of embezzlement, he'd managed to drop a landscaping timber on his foot and crush his thumb between two decorative rocks. After giving instructions to his employees to finish cleaning up around the Dolan home and haul everything back to the nursery, he pointed his truck toward Lydia's house and hit the gas.

Lydia's house. For all intents and purposes, Casey owned it now, but he had yet to make that transition. And no wonder. Lydia had only been gone a few weeks. The closest thing to a mother he ever really knew had disappeared as quickly as his birth mother. The vague memories of his real mom before the accident were replaced by Lydia's love and kindness. Now that had been wrenched from him.

Casey and Monah believed Carol was the culprit. Could it be true? He didn't really know Carol all that well. She'd worked for his dad as long as he could remember and had been nice enough over the years, but he'd sensed a wall around her that couldn't be penetrated. She rarely talked about herself. He had to wonder just how well his dad knew her.

He shook his head to rid himself of the thought. The

information they had dug up at the library presented doubts he didn't like, about both his dad and Carol. Should he tell his dad what they'd found? What if he already knew? Should he confront Carol about her past? He'd always thought Lydia and his dad enjoyed more than just a close friendship. What if an indiscretion with Carol had set the wheels of recent events in motion?

He turned into Lydia's driveway, slammed on the brakes, and ran both hands over his face, wishing the indecision and unrest could be wiped away as easily. The ache in his chest grew as he realized that if he'd worked himself into such a state, Casey had to be in turmoil. The thought propelled him out of the truck and up the porch steps. When she didn't answer right away, he tried the doorknob and found it unlocked.

"Casey?"

Silence followed the single echo of his voice. His heart twinged. She promised in the phone call this morning not to do anything about Carol until he could join her, or at the very least to let him know of her plans.

"Casey?"

"Up here."

The attic door gaped at him. He hurried toward it, coming to a stop in the entry. Once his eyes adjusted to the dim light, he spotted her sitting on a dingy sofa under a small window.

"Case?" Envelopes lay scattered around her on the floor and on her lap. Picking his way to the edge of the couch, he sat down next to her. A puff of dust rose and danced in the sunbeam streaming through the glass. But the cloud didn't disguise the look of torment on her face. Tears stained her lashes and the curve of her cheeks. He took her hand in his. "You okay?"

She held a sheet of paper out to him. "You ever seen these?"

"What are they?" He took it from her and read the first line. *My dearest Lydia*. "Love letters? From who?"

"Look at the signature."

He flipped to the back. "John?" He grabbed another paper from the sofa. Same signature. "They're all from my uncle?"

"I thought Aunt Liddy and your dad had something going." She picked up a letter from her lap. "But these are all dated a good twenty-some years ago. This one is almost twenty-six years old. Why would she have kept them?"

The date on his letter matched Casey's. "Uncle John died around twenty-three or twenty-four years ago. I guess Lydia took up with Dad sometime after John's death."

"Weird."

"Huh?"

She shrugged. "It just seems weird."

He scanned some of the words scrawled across the page. "Have you read these?"

"Every one of them."

"It's obvious my uncle loved her very much. Since there are so many letters, and Lydia kept all of them, I guess the feeling was mutual." He looked up at her. "Maybe my dad was just what she needed to get through her loss, and it became something more."

"I guess." She scooped up the letters and stuffed them back into the envelopes. "I don't know that I could do it."

"The heart is a funny thing sometimes, Case."

She smiled up at him. "Yeah, I know."

There it was again. That same lack of control, the hammering in his chest, and the strong desire to sweep her into his arms and never let go. Just like last night when he finally had to kiss her or die trying. Was the sweat dripping down his back from the stuffy heat of the attic or from fighting the urge to kiss her thoroughly?

He compromised with a quick peck on the lips then shoved to his feet. "What do you say we get out of here? I feel the need for something cold." He ignored the grin on her face and followed her to the kitchen. "What made you come looking for those letters anyway?"

"Richard."

"Who? Oh, wait. Your dad."

"If you want to call him that." She motioned toward a chair at the table, tossed the stack of letters on the counter, and reached for a glass. "Would you like water or something stronger? I think there's still some soda in the fridge."

"Water will be fine." Once she placed the glass in front of him, he took a couple of swallows and sat down. "So your dad wanted those letters?"

"No. He wanted the gun Aunt Liddy left for him. I found the letters searching for it." She fidgeted and pushed a crumb around the table with her finger. "He implied he came for more than the gun, that he wants to reconcile, but I told him I couldn't deal with that right now."

"And. . ."

"And what?"

He shrugged. "I don't know. It just sounded like there was an 'and' in there somewhere."

She slumped over the table and rested her chin on her hand. "I don't know that I can reconcile with him,

Luke. First of all, I don't even know him. I was barely more than a toddler when he left. He means no more to me than"—she waved a hand through the air—"well, than Jack. I don't really know him either."

"If that's the case, shouldn't it be easy to forgive him and move on? That's probably all he wants. . .forgiveness."

Her eyes shot up at him, her back rigid. "After what he put my mom through? You don't know how many nights I heard her crying herself to sleep." She gave her head a fierce shake. "No way. Mom loved him, and he turned his back without even one word all these years, till now. He doesn't deserve forgiveness."

He leaned forward and touched her forearm, praying for the right words. "I think I know a little of what you're going through, Casey. I had the same feelings years ago toward the person who killed my mom."

He slid his hand down and intertwined their fingers. "Lydia helped me through it, and she wasn't even a believer then. She said all my feelings of anger and bitterness were only hurting one person—me. She told me they'd eat a hole in me and steal my happiness. She warned me that letting go of the hurt wasn't an easy process, but I'd never truly heal until I could forgive."

Now for the difficult part. He took a deep breath. "I've not told anyone this before." Their eyes met, and the tears he saw forming in the corners of hers were almost his undoing. He swallowed hard and looked away. "I'm constantly asking forgiveness for my thoughts and feelings about my dad."

She squeezed his fingers. "What kind of thoughts?"

"Anger, resentment. He stopped loving me a long time ago."

She gasped and wrapped his hand in both of hers. "Of course he loves you, Luke. What makes you think he doesn't?"

"I don't think it, Case; I know it. We haven't been close since my mom died, at least, not as close. I think he blames me. I was in the car. Maybe he thinks I distracted her in some way, which led to the accident. Dad hasn't been the same since. And then he lost his brother right after Mom. It was probably more than he could bear."

Luke shrugged. "But I've learned to live with it. I think Lydia must have noticed, because she took up where he left off. We've had a lot of fun over the years." He smiled. "She was quite a lady. You're a lot like her, you know." He winked and leaned toward her. "But what I'm trying to say is, I've been where you are, many times, and I can help you get through it. Forgiveness is tough. It means you have to work through the hurt so you can heal. But the feeling of peace when you let it go is worth it. Trust me."

He put his arm around her and pulled her close.

She leaned into him. "Mom did forgive him, finally."

"And?"

She bumped him with her shoulder and smiled. "She seemed happier after that."

The front door slammed open. "Casey, I'm ba-ack." Monah's singsong voice reached them just before she appeared. She leaned against the door frame and propped a fist on her hip, her eyes spearing him as she frowned. "Since when did you stop waving to friends, Luke?"

"When did you wave?"

"I passed you on the road. You were headed this way. I even gave a blast on the horn. Nothing." She moved into the room and pushed a book toward Casey as she flopped into a chair. "Guess you had better things on your mind than paying attention to an old friend, eh?" Her eyebrows danced up and down as she grinned.

"Right." He kicked her under the table. "If I'd seen you, I would have swerved."

"Don't know it. I almost had a wreck the last time you did that." She nodded toward Casey, who was flipping through the pages of the book. "I glanced through that before I left the library. Check out the pictures of the rocks in the middle. There's a couple that look an awful lot like yours."

"What rocks?" He looked from one girl to the other.

Monah moved to the chair nearest Casey and dropped her finger on one of the pages. "Those right there."

He leaned closer to Casey and looked over her shoulder. "What rocks?"

"Oh my goodness." Casey pulled the book closer. "I think that's them."

"I know. Now go to the pages listed below the picture. This blew me away."

Luke growled. "What rocks?"

Monah peered around Casey. "We found some rocks in the box with Richard's gun. Casey said they looked just like the one she found in Lydia's shoe at the river."

"Oh?"

"Yeah, and you should have seen the look on Richard's face when he saw them. He couldn't get out of here fast enough."

Monah sometimes exaggerated when excited. Time for a second opinion. "Casey?"

She stuck a finger in the air to stop him, her lips moving while she read.

He dipped his head to find the title then frowned. "This book is about gemstones."

Casey gasped then grabbed his arm. "Oh man. This says that a shipment of raw gemstones was stolen somewhere between Africa and Boston and they've never been recovered. They figure the total value is around twelve million dollars." She looked up at Monah. "You don't think—?" She turned to him. "Surely Aunt Liddy didn't—?"

He snorted. "Steal? No way." The girls remained silent. He had to stop this. They were getting out of hand again. "Where are these stones?"

"I left them on the couch in the attic."

Monah jumped up. "I'll get them."

"Casey." He waited for her to look at him. "You don't really think Lydia stole those gemstones."

Her head dipped an inch. "No." She stared right through him. "But my dad seemed to recognize those rocks, and he worked at the Port of Boston." The book dropped to the table. "I think he could have done it."

17

The library was busy on Saturdays. Casey stood on the steps with Monah. Patrons rushed in and out, their chatter all but drowning out Monah's words.

A tear fell onto the picture frame clutched in Casey's hands. She wiped it away with her sleeve, letting her fingers linger over Aunt Liddy holding a cloud of cotton candy. Twinkling lights peppered the edges. Happy people filled the background. She'd probably recognize one or two if she looked hard enough.

She sighed and moved with Monah to a quiet spot on the library steps where a young tree heavy with new leaves shaded them from the morning sun. "Thanks for doing this. I mean it. You didn't have to go to so much trouble."

Monah smiled. "I figured while I was copying the photo, I might as well have it enlarged and framed. I'm glad you like it."

"I do. It's perfect. Thank you." She slid the picture into her shoulder bag. "So you sure you're okay researching the stones by yourself?"

Monah nodded. "I have to be here anyway. Maybe I'll get lucky and find out when the stones disappeared and what's been done to recover them."

"I'll call you later to see what you came up with."

"Sounds good. And let me know if anything interesting happens on your end."

After a quick good-bye, Casey continued down the library steps toward the rental car. She and Luke had agreed to keep an eye on Carol's activities. She glanced at her watch. He should be arriving any minute, and then the two of them would ride in the rental car, since Carol would be less likely to recognize it. It was a good plan. . .except that Luke had yet to appear, and Carol was climbing into her vehicle.

Where could she be going?

Frustrated, she tapped a rapid beat on the steering wheel. Luke had better hurry up, or they'd lose her and the whole day would be wasted. She breathed an agonized sigh as Carol eased from the curb and disappeared around the corner.

She couldn't let that happen—better to call Luke once she figured out where Carol was headed. A moment later, she eased into traffic. Luckily, Carol had been caught at the stoplight. Her white Camry waited just a few cars ahead. Casey settled into a spot several lengths back, the same way Brandy Purcell did when she tailed the killer in *Murder by the Letter*.

Several blocks and one stop sign later, Carol turned toward the highway. Casey waited long enough to avoid raising suspicion, then followed suit.

Wherever Carol was going, she was in a hurry. The speedometer read 78 miles per hour as Casey ducked between two semitrailers to keep from being seen. Half a mile later, Carol swung off the highway toward a rest area. Weaving through RVs, Casey found a space several yards from where she parked and shut off the engine.

Should I go inside?

Carol stepped from her car, a brown paper bag clutched under her arm. The wind tossed her hair as she hurried up the sidewalk toward the ladies' room.

Wrapped in indecision, Casey didn't even see the second figure until he smacked into Carol and sent the paper bag flying.

Detective Rafferty!

She slumped lower in the seat. What were the odds of running into him at a rest area several miles out of town? He helped Carol gather her things, and then the two of them separated, Carol continuing on toward the restroom and Rafferty toward his car.

Except he kept the bag.

Shocked, she stared at Carol. Didn't the woman realize what had happened? She sat up straight as Rafferty climbed into his car and tossed the bag onto the seat. He'd kept it on purpose!

She fumbled to turn the keys in the ignition. What business did Carol have with Rafferty, and what were they exchanging?

Casey followed Rafferty back out onto the highway. They drove all the way to Marlborough, to a white brick building lined with hedges and surrounded by tall maples.

The sign above the door swayed back and forth, pushed by a gentle breeze. " 'Sabine House,' " Casey read. "What is this place?"

The extra time it took to park left her hurrying to catch up with Rafferty. She passed several attendants along the way, but no one bothered to stop her as she scurried down a long tiled hall. Most doors stood open, and people lounged both in and out, some in robes and wheelchairs, others dressed in suits and ties. Antiseptic and the aroma of Italian spaghetti floated heavy on the air.

This place looks like a. . .

She snapped her fingers as Officer Brockman's words

came floating back to her. *"It's Saturday, and. . .well, he goes to visit his wife every week."*

Casey slowed. Which way had he gone? A second later, she spied him just as he disappeared into one of the rooms.

Curiosity prompted her to pick up a smock lying on a tray and jerk it over her head before easing toward the door.

"I like hamburgers. You know how I've always liked hamburgers." A woman's voice, tremulous and frail, drifted from inside the room.

Casey peeked inside. Rafferty and his wife sat at a small table in front of the window. An angel collection peered at them from the walls and shelves. The setting sun cast a yellow glow through the wings of one of the dolls. The shimmer made it come alive and gave life to its unnatural stare. Casey drew in a breath and backed up a step.

"So what's been happening, Judy? Anything you need me to help with?"

"Well," she replied, straightening a doily, "I wondered if you heard anything new. The woman, is she okay? Did she make it?"

Rafferty stiffened and jerked his head toward the door. Casey flattened to the wall. Had he seen her? She waited, afraid to move.

"Have you said anything to anyone? Tell me, Judy."

At Rafferty's rough words, Casey dared breathe. She shouldn't eavesdrop. It was wrong, but she had to know what woman Judy referred to. She strained to listen.

"You told me not to. You know I always try to do like you ask."

Weariness rang in Rafferty's deep sigh. "Yeah, I know."

"I'm so glad you're here. I've missed you, darling." Judy's voice turned pleading. "Can't I go home this time?"

"You know what the doctor said."

"But I'm better now. I haven't asked anyone about...you know. Not once, I swear. The dolls are the only thing I talk about in my sessions."

Silence throbbed through the room and hallway. What were they doing? Much as she wanted to know, Casey didn't dare risk another look. She waited, adrenaline plucking at every nerve.

"Is the woman okay? Did she make it?"

"Judy—"

"I have to know! Is she dead? Did I kill her? I didn't mean to. The car just got away from me. Tell me, William. Please, tell me."

Quiet sobbing filled the hall. Casey froze, heart pounding. Aunt Liddy. Judy Rafferty killed Aunt Liddy and Rafferty covered it up to protect his wife. It had to be. Who else could she be talking about? A slow rage built in the pit of her stomach.

"She's dead, isn't she?"

"Yes."

"So I really did do it?"

She had to look. Casey swung her head toward the entrance. Huge tears filled Judy's eyes and ran down her cheeks.

Judy grabbed Rafferty's hand. "I didn't mean to. She came right at me."

"It's all right, Judy. Calm down. It was an accident."

"But I killed her." She snatched a tissue from the box on the window ledge and dabbed at her eyes. "I can't live with this." She blew her nose. "Maybe I should talk to her family. Explain what happened and apologize. Has there been a funeral yet? Maybe I should go."

"Like I've told you many times before, it's best you stay here and keep quiet. I've taken care of everything. All you have to do is stay put and don't tell anyone about the accident. You do remember that you promised not to say a word, don't you?"

She picked up the little angel figurine on the table, rubbing its head with her thumb. "We've talked about this before?"

A young orderly rounded the corner, but he was so preoccupied with the chart in his hands, he barely gave Casey a glance. Rafferty shushed his wife as the worker passed by the door.

"Keep your voice down. You'll only upset yourself."

"And the boy, what about him? I saw him in the backseat, but I couldn't bring myself to pull him from the wreckage. There was too much blood, and I thought. . .I just thought. . ." Her voice rose with every word.

"For crying out loud, it was twenty-four years ago! Why can't you let it go?"

Muffled sniffles replaced Judy's agonized weeping. A clock on the wall chimed the hour. Casey fought to quiet her breathing.

"Why can't you just let it go?" Rafferty repeated softly. "I've done everything I know to do. I've tried so hard to protect you, and still. . ."

Casey pressed her back to the wall, tears brimming in her eyes. Of course. The woman they were talking about couldn't have been Aunt Liddy. Officer Brockman said Judy Rafferty had been ill for years. Rafferty wasn't a killer, but he was a liar, and he'd spent a good portion of his life covering up his wife's mistake.

"Look, I've got to go."

Jerking her head back, Casey scanned the hall for the nearest exit.

"You just got here," Judy said.

"I know, but I was already running late, and I still have some work to finish."

"I won't mention her anymore. And they're just about to serve dinner. Hamburgers. You know how I like hamburgers."

Sickened, Casey tore off the smock and stumbled out of the passageway into the parking lot. She climbed into the car and drove out onto the highway. Luke—she had to find him and figure out a way to tell him that she'd uncovered the person responsible for his mother's death.

18

Luke sat in Lydia's driveway, his bouncing leg jiggling the keys still hanging from the truck's ignition. A box of fries sat in a congealed mass next to his half-eaten hamburger. Where was Casey? She said to meet him at the house, but that was half an hour ago. The way she drove, he thought she'd surely be the one waiting on him. And what was with her tone of voice? Fear? Nervousness? He couldn't tell, but it put a twist in his stomach that hadn't yet straightened out. •

They'd staked out Carol's house every night. After days of nothing but the usual, something must have happened today, and on the one day he ran late meeting up with Casey.

Tires crunched on the gravel drive. Casey pulled to a stop behind him. He shot out of the truck and helped her from her car. She didn't meet his eyes. Not a good sign.

"You okay?"

She took his hand and led the way to the house. "Let's go inside."

His stomach twisted a little tighter. "Sorry I was late. Cat trouble."

She cast a glance over her shoulder. "Did another one d—"

"Die? No. I just had to chase it out of the greenhouse."

She motioned to the couch. He sat, but she kept walking. *Pacing* was a better description. And she chewed on her thumbnail. If she didn't have him so on edge, he would have laughed.

"What's wrong, Case? You lose your Post-it pad?"

She paused long enough to cast him a slight smirk then continued her pacing.

No snappy comeback. This was bad. "What happened? Did Carol say or do something you're afraid to tell me?"

She stopped and stared at him. Tears formed in her eyes as she moved to sit beside him. Instead of getting comfortable, she remained leaning forward.

"I guess the beginning is the best place to start."

"Usually." They might finally be getting somewhere.

She turned toward him. "I couldn't wait for you, Luke. If I had, Carol would have gotten away."

"I figured as much."

She licked her lips, her fingers winding round and round a flowing lock of hair. "I followed her to the interstate. I thought maybe she was taking a trip for the weekend, but she pulled into the rest area and headed toward the ladies' room." She touched his knee. "This is where it gets weird. Rafferty ran into her and knocked everything from her hands."

"Rafferty?"

She nodded. "He helped her pick it all up but kept a small brown bag. Carol went into the ladies' room, but Rafferty tossed the bag into his car and left. I didn't know what else to do, so I followed him instead of waiting for Carol."

"I would have done the same. Where did he go?"

Again she looked away, clasping and unclasping her intertwined fingers. "We ended up in Marlborough. A place called Sabine House. Have you heard of it?"

"Doesn't sound familiar."

He could hear her swallow. Whatever she was about to tell him had her more than a little upset.

"It's some kind of nursing home or something. Almost like an institution, I guess."

"And Rafferty went inside?"

"Yeah, and I followed him."

He leaned up next to her. "Case—"

"It was okay. He didn't see me."

He shook his head. What was he going to do with her? She took too many risks. "Okay. Then what?"

"I heard him talking to his wife. She sounded so weak and fragile." She turned on the couch to face him and took his hand in both of hers. "Luke, what she said. . ."

Her bottom lip quivered. She caught it between her teeth. Luke hesitated. This was about him. If it were about her, she would be crying and letting the problem spew forth. What she had to say would be painful, and she didn't want to hurt him. His heart swelled at the same time that his gut twisted.

"What did she say, Case?"

Her gaze fell. "She said something about losing control of her car and asked if the lady was dead."

Was she talking about Lydia? He frowned. "What lady?"

Casey squeezed his hand and looked him dead in the eyes. "She also asked about the little boy in the backseat."

The image of his mother smiling at him from his favorite photograph flashed through his mind then blurred. Little boy in the backseat.

He dropped against the sofa back and stared straight ahead. The accident. She'd killed his mom.

"Luke."

He stood and walked to the window. Rafferty had known all this time but never said a word. Burning anger traveled up to his throat and threatened to choke him. Every muscle in his body grew taut, begging for release.

Help me, Lord. Before I do something I regret, help me.

"Luke." The touch of Casey's hand on his back was like ice to a flame. She took his clenched fist in her other hand. "I'm so sorry." She stepped around and looked up into his face. Tears rimmed her lashes. "I don't know if it will help, but Mrs. Rafferty spoke as though it just happened, like she hasn't moved past that day. I think that's why she's in that home. I think it affected her mind."

"And Rafferty? What's his excuse?" He relaxed his hand and grasped hers. "He's the one who found me, Case." His throat tightened. "He said he came upon the accident by chance while doing his patrol. But all this time, he's been covering his wife's tracks."

The rage roared back to life. "Do you think he's still there? You think I can catch him?"

"Luke."

"They need to pay, Casey."

She grabbed him by the arms. He almost shrugged her away, until he saw the pain in her eyes.

"I know how you feel, but you need to slow down and think first. I've been where you are, Luke, and to strike out in anger is a mistake."

She pulled him into a hug, her head against his chest. He couldn't bring himself to respond, much as he wanted to. She stepped back and met his gaze, her lips quivering.

"Let's sit down and talk a little bit before you decide what to do."

He didn't want to talk. He wanted to confront the two people who had changed his life forever. . .who had placed a wedge between him and his dad. He wanted to let everyone know their detective was a fake. Instead, he allowed Casey to lead him back to the couch, his hand firmly in hers. Like a stone, he dropped next to her, feeling just as hard and cold. His mind grasped for something to grab on to. All the advice he'd given Casey about forgiveness came rolling back.

Lord, help me.

He closed his eyes, searching for the help and peace the Lord promised to those who sought Him. The peace he requested arrived in slow increments, like a seedling taking root and coming to life. He allowed the calm to wash over him and fill the empty places. Though the pain remained, he let go of the anger.

Thank you, Lord.

"You okay?"

He opened his eyes. Casey's face hovered only inches from his. She moved back a bit when he smiled.

"I am now."

Again she examined his eyes. "You were praying, weren't you?"

He nodded. "I didn't know what else to do. I went where I knew I could find help."

A puzzled frown marred her smooth features. "Monah said something similar the other day. And Mom was like that before she died. She spent a lot of time in prayer." She tugged impatiently at a strand of her hair. "I wish I found the same comfort in it that you all seem to. I mean, I've accepted Christ, but sometimes I wonder if He hears."

Luke took her hand in his and brought it to his lips. "He hears us, Case. I don't know how anyone can get through tough times without the Lord. I'm glad I don't have to try."

After giving him another long once-over, a smile played at the corners of her mouth. "Good. So did you decide what to do now?"

"I think I should talk to Dad. He needs to know. It might be more his decision than mine on how to proceed."

She stared until he squirmed.

"What?"

"Praying really did help, didn't it? You're like a totally different man." She leaned in and gave him a quick kiss. "And you're right. You need to tell your dad."

He wanted to make sure she understood. "I'm human, Casey. I'm still hurt and upset, but anger doesn't do God or me a bit of good. He helped me with that, just as I know He'll help me through the rest." He stood and held out his hand. "Come to Dad's with me?"

She took it. "Are you sure? This is kind of a private matter between the two of you."

"I can't think of anyone I'd rather have with me." Without a doubt. Just her presence was like a balm.

They left after calling his dad to make sure they'd find him at home. The news she'd just shared with him played through his mind on the way into town, this time without the anger, and he was better able to give it serious thought. Now he wanted to know more. He needed details.

"Tell me everything. Not only what you heard but your impressions. I need to know it all."

"There's not much more to tell." She stared off into space for a minute. "She asked if she could go home. Rafferty said no. He sounded sad."

Over twenty years without his wife. Even Rafferty would have to feel some kind of sorrow. At least he would think so.

"Then when Judy kept asking—"

"Judy?"

"That's what he called her."

"Okay." He turned onto his dad's street and slowed, not yet ready to give him the news.

"When she kept asking if the woman, um, your mom was dead, Rafferty yelled at her. Asked her why she couldn't just let it go. Then he sounded sad again."

"I would imagine after dealing with this same thing over and over for so many years, it would be frustrating and depressing at the same time." He forced himself to try to understand, but compassion for the couple had yet to find its way into his heart.

His dad's house came into view, and he eased to a stop in the driveway then sat staring at the front door. How to tell him? And how would he take the news? After a quick prayer for strength and wisdom, he pushed out the door and met Casey in front of the truck. She slipped her hand in his and gave a squeeze. She was with him, more than just physically, and he smiled in appreciation.

Before they could get to the door, his dad had it opened and motioned them inside.

"Well, Casey. I didn't expect this pleasure. Luke never said a word." His gaze switched to Luke. "You sounded a little tense on the phone. Anything wrong? Business trouble?"

The last question hit him like a fist. His dad would just love for him to have business trouble. Then there would be no excuse not to work for him.

"My business is doing fine." He sat on the couch but couldn't even try to relax. The news would be hard enough to tell without this added strain.

His dad sat in the leather recliner across from him. "I'm sorry, son. I just—" He shrugged, crossed his legs, and brushed at his trousers. "I'm sorry."

That was a first. He couldn't remember his dad ever apologizing before. But it certainly melted the tension. He sat back and absorbed some strength from Casey's touch.

"Dad, I'm afraid I've got some news."

"Oh?"

Luke squirmed. How to say this? How to start?

"It's all right, son. Out with it."

He leaned forward, rested his forearms on his legs, and met his dad's eyes. "I know who killed Mom."

The silence stretched on for several moments.

His dad got up, poured himself a ginger ale from the dry bar, and resumed his seat in the recliner. "Who?"

How could he be so calm? "Rafferty's wife. Casey heard her talking to the detective about the accident. Even asked about the little boy in the backseat." And how did he manage to state it so matter-of-factly?

Not a scowl. Not even a twitch. Had the years dulled his love to the point that it no longer existed? That he no longer cared?

"Judy Rafferty, huh? You know that for a fact?"

"Everything she said points to it."

"She said your mom's name?"

He glanced at Casey, who shook her head. "Well, no, but—"

"Don't go accusing someone until you're sure, Luke. You'll only stir up trouble and cause hurt feelings."

He fought to tamp down the anger and frustration igniting within. Only Casey's hand on his back kept him calm.

"Rafferty himself said the accident happened twenty-four years ago. That makes me sure."

His dad ran the crease in his pants between thumb and finger, casting glances at him from time to time. "I see."

Muscles bunching from the tension, it was all he could do to sit still. What was wrong with him? Were there no feelings left at all for Mom and what had happened? "So what do you intend to do about it?"

"Do?" He shrugged.

Luke stood. "What's wrong with you? Don't you care anymore?"

"Luke—" His dad stood with him.

"I know it's been a long time, but surely you feel something."

"Luke, I know Judy is in a home. Has been for years."

He stopped pacing and stared. "You knew?"

"I only knew she was in a home. I didn't know she caused the accident."

Well, that was something.

"But if the accident caused her mental disorder, don't you think she's been through enough?"

"I wasn't talking about her. It's Rafferty I'm after. He's lied all these years. He's a detective—one who should lose his job."

"Now hold on a minute, son." His dad reached for him. Luke shrugged away. With a helpless gesture, his dad took a step closer. "He lost his wife. And he's led an honest life since then. Maybe it's enough to just let it go."

Luke walked to the fireplace and stared at the mantel clock, the second hand showing how fast time slipped away, never to be recaptured. Was he blowing everything out of proportion? Was his dad right? "So you condone what Rafferty's done?" He whirled to see his dad's face when he answered, searching for remorse, pain on his father's face, agonized to discover it wasn't there.

"I could never condone it." He jammed his hands into his pockets and rocked onto his toes as keys and change jingled. "But maybe it's time to forgive and let life move on."

"Life has gone on, and I've moved with it." He returned to stand in front of his dad. "But I also believe that the public needs to know. . .deserves to know what kind of man they have on the police force."

His dad sighed. "You don't think he's been punished enough, what with all he has to face with his wife?"

Luke looked out the window over his dad's shoulder, his emotions swaying between frustration and sympathy. Charity wasn't forthcoming. Was it because his dad seemed too charitable? Where were the shock and feelings of outrage that had struck him when he first heard the truth?

"What do you think your mom would want you to do, Luke?"

The question slammed him in the chest. He clenched his jaw and looked at his dad. "I wouldn't know. I didn't have her long enough to find out." He turned to Casey. "I'm ready to leave."

She stood and walked with him to the door, her face pale.

His dad trailed behind. "Son, wait. Let me ponder on it some more. You've had more time to think about it. Just give me some time."

He grabbed the knob. "Too much time has gone by already. You've grown immune to the pain and loss. Your only thoughts are of the Raffertys. Maybe if Mom still meant something to you, you'd be a little more willing to do something in her memory."

Their gazes met and held, and what Luke didn't see in his dad's eyes raised the wall between them even higher. All the years he'd wished they had a closer relationship seemed to end with the shutting of the front door, and his heart ached as never before.

19

Silence roared inside the truck cab. Casey risked a peek at Luke's hard profile, dimly lit by the glow of the dash and glimmer of twilight. Sorrow jerked inside her chest at the pain she read in the tense line of his jaw.

"I'm sorry."

His nostrils flared. "Thanks."

"Anything I can do?"

White-knuckled, he shook his head. Somehow, she sensed he needed someone to listen, not offer advice. She closed her mouth and waited.

"Mom loved flowers."

The headlights of a passing car illumined the tears glistening in his eyes. Why didn't he just let them fall? She turned in the seat to face him. "Did she?"

"I order a bouquet sent to the cemetery on special occasions."

The floral receipt. Casey suddenly recalled finding it under the truck seat.

"I remember trudging through the muddy garden after her. Both of us got filthy, but she didn't care." Shadowed by grief, a tiny smile tugged at his lips and disappeared. "I loved the smell of dirt on my fingers when I was a kid. I figured it had to taste good. She never could break me from eating it. Maybe if she'd lived longer."

Casey laughed and leaned close to lay her hand on his shoulder. "I'm honored. I bet you don't tell that to just anybody."

After a moment, he joined in her laughter. Relieved

to see the tension leave his body, she reached for his hand. "Are you okay?"

He squeezed her fingers. "I will be. I just can't understand. . . I mean, I feel sorry for the Raffertys, too, but does that excuse them from facing the consequences of their actions?" He pulled his hand away to slap the steering wheel. "People think that because Christians are commanded to forgive, they aren't supposed to pursue justice, but that's not true, Case. My mom. . .the way she died. . . Do you know how long I heard her screams in my nightmares? And Dad—"

Her heart throbbed in sympathy. "We'll figure it out, Luke." Several cars zoomed past while she waited for him to look at her. He did, at last. "We'll figure it out."

Anger drained from his face and left him pale. He nodded. Glad when the rooftop of Aunt Liddy's house came into view, Casey touched Luke's forearm. "Come inside. We'll talk about what to do next."

He didn't argue. Once in the driveway, he stepped from the truck and circled around to help her out.

"Are you hungry?" She pulled the keys from her purse and unlocked the front door.

"Later."

Understandable. Despite the hour, she couldn't eat anything either. "Let's go into the kitchen. I'll fix coffee." She flipped on lights as they walked. "You realize that apart from the crime against your family, there's still something we haven't touched on."

He followed her to the cupboard and rummaged for the coffee tin while she filled the pot with water. "Carol."

"Right. What was she doing with Rafferty, and what was in the bag?"

"You think maybe Carol was blackmailing him? Maybe she found out about his wife."

Casey switched the coffeemaker on. "No. If that were the case, Rafferty would have been bringing the bag to her, not the other way around."

"Okay, let's assume it was money in the bag. So what does Rafferty have on Carol?" He leaned against the counter as the aroma of brewing coffee wafted through the kitchen.

She tapped her finger to her temple. Odd as Rafferty and Carol had looked together, she'd seen them before, but where?

"What are you thinking?"

Her hand fell. "I can't get the picture of Rafferty and Carol out of my head. I keep thinking. . ." She snapped her fingers. "That's it. The picture."

She hurried to the rental car and retrieved the photo Monah had enlarged for her from the front seat. Her breathing shallow, she rushed back inside and held it toward him. "See anything interesting?" Luke's fingers closed around hers for a brief second as he took the frame. "It's the picture from the memorial service, the one Monah said you liked."

"In the background. What do you see?"

His eyes narrowed. She knew the moment he saw it. His brows rose, and he drew a sharp breath. "Is that—?"

"Carol and Rafferty. There are other people around, of course, but those two are definitely together. Look at the way their bodies are turned, almost like they're whispering."

"And Carol is staring at Lydia."

"What?"

"Look." He held the frame out for her to see.

She traced Carol's figure with her finger. "You could be right. You know, I noticed her staring at Jack the other day at the memorial." She froze.

He gripped her arm. "What's the matter?"

She tipped her head to stare at him. "What if we have it wrong? What if it wasn't Carol who found out about Rafferty's wife?"

"Huh?"

"All right, I'm brainstorming here, but let's say Aunt Liddy uncovered Rafferty's dirty secret and threatened to expose him. It makes sense, Luke. Remember the debt Aunt Liddy said she owed you in her will? Maybe she felt guilty for not going to the police sooner. Now the question is, would Rafferty be desperate enough to kill her in order to stop her?"

"But what about Carol? Why would she be helping. . ." He slapped his forehead. "The embezzling."

"What?"

"The article we found said she was arrested. It didn't say anything about her serving time."

"We just didn't search far enough. I'm sure she went to jail."

"Unless the charges were dropped."

"Why would that happen?"

"Maybe somebody got her off—someone inside the police department? A cover-up?"

"In exchange for favors!"

"Uh-huh."

"Oh my, Luke. I think we're onto something."

He rubbed both hands over his face. "Okay, let's slow down and think about this for a minute." He gestured toward the table.

She followed, the chairs scraping on the tiled floor as they sat. From a pocket in her purse, she pulled a Post-it pad and pencil. "Here's what we know. One"—she scribbled on the sheet, tore it off, and stuck it to the table—"Rafferty's wife is responsible for your mom's accident. Two"—more scribbling—"Rafferty found out and covered it up. Three, and this is a guess, Carol somehow knew all of this and has been helping him keep it a secret." In her excitement, she snapped the lead on her pencil. "Drat!"

"Hold on. I think I have one here somewhere." He dug through his jacket pocket. Along with a calculator, he laid some change, a stick of gum, and a crumpled napkin on the table. "Here it is." He handed her a mechanical pencil, complete with eraser.

A grin forming, Casey stared at the napkin, where a piece of silver metal stuck out. "You wear a retainer?"

"What?"

She pointed. "Is that a retainer?"

He grimaced. "No. That's something one of Mrs. Teaser's cats hacked up. I've been meaning to give it to my dad, since she said she found it at his house, but I keep forgetting."

The grin faded. "So what is it?"

"Take a look."

She peeled back the napkin to reveal a partial with two yellowed teeth. "Ick! You mean the cat swallowed that?"

"Yep."

Her mouth went dry. "And Mrs. Teaser found it at your dad's house."

"Uh-huh."

A wave of nausea swept over her. "Luke?"

His brow furrowed with concern. "Yeah?"

"I don't think Rafferty killed Aunt Liddy."

20

For the space of a full heartbeat, neither of them spoke.

Sweat dampened Casey's palms. She rubbed them on her pant legs. "Luke, is your dad missing any teeth?"

He frowned in bewilderment. "What does that have to do with anything?"

"Is he?"

"I don't think so. Why?"

"Because. . .he should be."

"What on earth are you talking about?"

She rose, sadness for him enveloping her. "Wait here a minute."

"Casey—"

"I'll be right back."

The stairs creaked as she climbed them. The feeble light of the dim bulb hanging in the closet made it difficult to see, but she found what she sought at last and walked back into the kitchen.

Luke paced the floor. "What's going on, Case?"

Her hand shook as she passed him the picture she'd found of Jack and John as young boys.

"What is this?"

She pointed to one of the boys. "Your father. Check out his smile."

The muscles in Luke's jaw stood out in stark relief. "I've never seen this before. Are you sure it's him?"

"Turn it over. Someone, possibly your grandmother, wrote the names and date on the back, as well as how he lost his teeth."

"What are you saying? Are you implying that my father—that he's not my dad?"

Nerves screaming, she nodded. "Remember the bones? The skull was missing teeth."

"That's not—" He sank into a chair next to the table. "I can't believe it."

She plopped down next to him. "Think about it. Unless he somehow grew new teeth, the man you've assumed is your father isn't Jack at all. He's John."

"But"—he laid the picture down next to the one of Aunt Liddy and took hold of her hand—"that means Lydia. . ."

Truth dawned like a kick to Casey's gut. The blood drained from her face in a quick rush. "Aunt Liddy would have known. She loved him."

"She helped him cover it up? All these years, and she never said a word?"

"The debt she owed you." Her whispered statement hung like a noose between them.

With a deep, shuddering breath, Luke drew back and shook his head. "No. What about Rafferty and Carol? I still think it could have been them."

She placed her hand on his arm. "Perhaps. . .no." She picked up the photo. "This was at the Fall Festival, months before Aunt Liddy disappeared. That means the two of them were conspiring together long before she disappeared."

He jerked to his feet. "No! I can't believe it. There's no way she carried this secret all these years."

Tears soaked her hands as she pressed them to her cheeks. "Love makes people do crazy things, Luke."

His fingers tore through his hair. "Okay, say you're

right. Say my father died, and John and Lydia covered it up. Are we suggesting that John killed his own brother? Why? What happened between them?"

She shook her head. "I don't know."

"And there's still the question of Carol and Rafferty. What about them?"

"I suspect we're going to find the two crimes are unrelated." She rose from the table and went to stand next to him. "All along, we've been assuming that these things were somehow tied together, but what if they're not?"

By the line of concentration creasing his forehead, she knew he was mulling things over. "You might be right. It would explain so much."

"What do you mean?"

"How much do you suppose it costs Rafferty to keep his wife in an institution, away from anyone who knows her and might recall what happened all those years ago?"

She shrugged. "I have no idea. A lot?"

"Oh yeah. More than a detective makes in a year. So where does he get the money?"

"The bag."

"Right."

"So you think Rafferty got Carol out of jail, and she's been paying him off ever since."

He nodded. "Probably with money she's been stealing from work."

She waved her hand in the air. "Wait, let's just think this over for a minute." Turning from the sink, she paced to the refrigerator and back, coming to a stop in front of him. "That brings us back to Jack and John. We don't know what caused the fight between them, but even so, that doesn't explain what happened to Aunt Liddy."

"Maybe it does."

She shrank away from the terrible truth she saw gleaming in his eyes until she felt the countertop press into her spine. "He killed her." It wasn't a question. She already knew.

His slow nod confirmed it.

"Because after she became a Christian. . .she could no longer bear keeping their horrible secret and threatened to go to the police. It must have eaten at her for months." Sobs fractured her words so they crumbled and fell like bricks.

His arms wrapped around her like a warm blanket. "Yes."

"Oh, Luke. How awful." She shuddered and felt his strong body press closer to hers.

"I'm sorry, Casey. I'm so sorry."

The kisses he pressed to the top of her head comforted as no words could have. The ringing of her cell phone startled them both.

She glanced at the caller ID. "It's Monah. She's probably calling to let me know what she found out about the gems."

A second later, the doorbell echoed the cell phone's ringing.

"Could you get that?"

He paused long enough to wipe the tears from her cheeks and then went to answer.

She turned from the door and flipped open the phone on the sixth ring. "Monah?"

"Hey, Casey. How'd it go today?"

"You wouldn't believe me if I told you. How about you?"

"Not so good. The gemstones stolen from the Port of Boston were never recovered, but other than that, nothing. It's like the silly things just disappeared."

Casey plucked at her lip. "And yet these rocks showed up in Aunt Liddy's possession."

"Weird, huh?"

Sighing, she pressed her palm to her forehead. "Yeah. Okay, I've got a lot to catch you up on, but I suppose it'll have to wait until morning. Can you come by before church?"

"Sure. Seven o'clock good?"

"Fine. I'll see you tomorrow."

"Bye, Casey."

"Bye—hey, Monah, wait." Struck with an idea, Casey straightened. "Do you think your mother might know of a reason why John, I mean Jack, why the two of them may have quarreled? I mean really fought?"

"Goodness, I don't know. I could ask her."

"Would you? And maybe let me know when you stop by in the morning?"

"You got it."

"Thanks, Monah. I'll talk to you tomorrow." She disconnected, laid the phone on the counter, and reached up to rub her aching shoulders.

"I might know of something."

She whirled.

Luke stood in the doorway with Richard, his face marked with chagrin. "Sorry, Casey. Your dad asked to see you. We couldn't help but overhear."

She couldn't be angry with Luke, not after everything he'd suffered the last few hours. "It's okay." She glanced at her father. "What are you doing here, Richard?"

"I came to see you." He stepped forward but stopped when she shot him a glare; then he shoved his hands into his pockets. "You're looking for something that happened between Jack and John?"

She didn't want to share what they knew with a man she distrusted, but if he really did know something. . . She nodded. "It would have been a long time ago, over twenty years."

He gave a slow nod and crossed to the table. "May I?"

She gestured for him to sit.

"Will you join me? Luke, you, too. I have a story I think you'll find very interesting, and it involves you both."

They glanced at each other and moved to sit across from him.

"Well?" Irritation built in Casey's chest. Why did Richard suddenly seem so eager to help?

He cleared his throat. "Is that coffee I smell?"

She filled a cup, set it down in front of him, and folded her arms. "Get to it." Jaw squared, she braced for whatever he was about to say.

His shoulders slumped, but he nodded. "I used to work at the Port of Boston. You were probably too young to remember." When she didn't answer, he continued. "I had been working there a couple of years. Bit by bit, I climbed my way up until I got a job filing manifests. One night, a man came to me. A powerful man. I could tell by the clothes he wore." He directed a look at Luke. "Your father."

The real Jack. Casey cast Luke a quick glance, desperately hoping he wasn't about to receive more bad news about his family.

Luke's fists clenched. "And?"

"He asked to see a manifest. It was illegal, but he paid me very well, and I needed the money."

"So you showed him?" Under the table, Casey slid her hand to Luke's knee.

"Yeah."

"What was in it?"

"Everything he needed to know about a shipment that was supposed to come into the port the next day, one ordered by his brother, John. He wanted me to lie and tell John it wouldn't come until days later."

Luke passed her a glance. "Do you know what was in it?"

Richard fidgeted in his chair. He tugged at the collar of his shirt and used a handkerchief pulled from his pocket to wipe his brow. "It was. . . The box contained"— he dropped his gaze, misery twisting his features—"raw gemstones. I know because I stole some of them. I figured it had to be something big for Jack Kerrigan to pay so much for information on its arrival. I took the money he paid me and as many gems as I thought I could get away with, and I ran." He lifted pain-filled eyes to Casey's. "I'm sorry, sweetheart. I was a weak fool. I threw away the best things that had ever happened to me for a few thousand dollars and a handful of stolen rocks. I've regretted it ever since."

The sorrow in his voice proved more than she could bear. Casey rose and walked over to the sink to peer out into the darkened garden. The pale light of the moon illuminated the yellow police tape marking one corner of the yard. It would stay there until the results from the forensic report came back.

"So," Luke said, "John hooked up with someone to snatch these gemstones as they were being transported from Africa. Jack found out about it and stole the shipment before John had a chance to get them."

"I believe that's what happened, yes."

"And when John found out what Jack had done, the two of them fought, probably at the house."

"I'm not sure."

Casey turned from the sink. "What?"

"I left town after that, so I can't say for certain what happened between the two brothers."

"But I think it would be safe to draw that conclusion," Luke said.

"And maybe another one." Both men shifted to look at her. She pushed a lock of hair behind her ear. "John was angry enough to kill Jack over what happened, but after the deed was done, he probably feared he'd be sent to prison, so he assumed his brother's identity." She swallowed hard against the bitter anguish roiling in her stomach. "With Aunt Liddy's help, he buried Jack in the garden and told everyone later that John died in a boating accident. It worked for a long time, until Aunt Liddy couldn't stand the secret anymore and threatened to go to the police. Faced with incarceration, John killed her and forged the suicide note to turn away suspicion."

To her surprise, Richard rose and crossed to stand beside her. "If that's true, you may be in more danger than you thought. I'm worried about you, Casey. I couldn't bear for something to happen to you after all this time. Promise me you'll be careful."

She stared at him. Genuine concern shone from his eyes, along with a glimmer of something else she could only assume was regret. Her chest tightened. "I will."

He broke the connection at last. "I'd better be going. Will you go to the police with the information I gave you?"

She glanced at Luke, who shook his head. "It's late, and tomorrow is Sunday. We may want to wait until Monday. Maybe by then the autopsy results will be back and we'll be able to prove beyond a doubt what happened."

She nodded quick agreement.

"Are you sure? What about John?"

Luke rose and crossed to drape his arm around Casey's shoulders. "He's not going anywhere without his money, and the bank doesn't open until Monday. I'll keep a close eye on your daughter to be sure nothing happens to her."

Your daughter.

Despite everything that had happened, she was Richard's daughter. She looked at her father and for the first time wasn't eaten with anger. "I'll be okay. Thanks for your help tonight."

She didn't pull away as he reached out to squeeze her hand. "Whatever you need me to do. Count on it." He gave her one last squeeze and turned to go.

Once he'd gone, she exhaled long and hard. "We've done it. I can't believe we've finally figured out what happened."

"Looks like." Luke drew her into a tight hug. "Telling John about the bones never entered my mind while we were there earlier. I guess it's a good thing."

She tipped her head back to look into his face. "Are we right to wait until Monday?"

He nodded. "I think so. In the meantime, you'd better find me a blanket. And call Monah back."

"Why?"

"I plan on being a permanent resident on your couch until all of this is settled." He tilted her chin up with his finger. "And you. . .are going to need a chaperone."

21

Luke gripped the steering wheel, his knuckles white. The nervous tension radiating through him didn't add any weight to the foot pressing on the gas pedal. His truck chugged down the road toward town behind Monday morning traffic.

Casey was in the same condition. Her teeth gnawed at her bottom lip, and her hands plucked at her fingernails. He rested his arm along the back of the seat and touched her shoulder.

"You okay with this?" He would have offered to meet with Rafferty alone just to save her from further pain but knew she wouldn't agree. She had just as much at stake as he did. Today might be the day she found out where Lydia's body lay.

She took his hand and turned in the seat. "I was wondering the same thing about you." Her bottom lip trembled. "You lost both parents, and now you'll lose your uncle. He'll go to jail, Luke."

The same thought had kept him awake all night. He turned his eyes to the road. "I know. But if he killed Dad, then justice is needed. Since I'm pretty sure he killed Lydia, too, he hasn't learned a thing except to continue murdering to cover his crimes. He has to be stopped."

Sorrow jabbed his chest. How could he still love someone and feel guilty for turning him in even now after learning what his uncle was capable of? There was certainly a good dose of anger involved, yet a part of him ached, knowing what he was about to do.

The discovery of what John had done certainly explained a lot of things, such as why his dad had changed so much after his wife's and brother's deaths. And why he didn't have a strong reaction when he learned about who killed Luke's mom. He couldn't experience strong emotions for someone he didn't even love.

He glanced at Casey and squeezed her hand. "What about you? You've lost just as much. Lydia died trying to make things right."

She swiveled her head to look out the side window, and he knew she fought pain of her own. He wanted, no, needed to hold her. "Hey," he said, clicking the button to unlock her seat belt, "come over here."

She turned her red-rimmed eyes toward him. He smiled and patted the seat. She slid over and buckled back in. Once she was settled, he pulled her close and kissed her temple.

"Too many times we focus on forgetting, when none of the scriptures talk about that. Remember what Pastor said yesterday? 'Forgiveness is not about forgetting. It's about letting go of the hurt.' We shouldn't hold a grudge, but we should remember so that we don't place ourselves in a position to be hurt in the same manner again."

She snuggled close, her body not quite so tense. "Yeah, that was a great message. I felt like he was talking right to me."

He chuckled. "I know what you mean. Pastor Burgess's messages have a way of hitting home."

They reached the edge of town, and he took the long way around to check on Monah. After filling her in Saturday night on all they'd learned, they decided someone needed to keep an eye on John. He'd been out of town for a week but had more than likely heard the news about the bones once he'd returned. The risk that he'd flee was too great. Since Monah had the day off, she'd volunteered to watch his every move. They spotted her on a side street across from John's office and waved. She gave them a thumbs-up.

Minutes later, the police station loomed in front of them. Luke found a parking spot near the front and shut off the engine, and they both stared in silence at the building. Today, lives would change, and they would be the instigators.

He reached for her hand. "You ready?"

"No. But let's get it over with."

His cell phone rang as he opened the truck door. A quick glance at the display screen made his heart thud. "It's Monah." He punched the RECEIVE button. "Everything okay?"

"He's on the move, Luke. I don't know where he's going yet, but he's in a hurry."

He motioned for Casey to get out. "All right. Keep us informed. We're on our way into the station now."

"You got it."

After turning off the phone and locking his truck, he took Casey's arm and rushed inside. "Monah said Dad, uh, John has left the office. Time to get things moving."

Rafferty sat in his office engrossed in a file, which he closed and set aside the moment he saw them. The scowl on his face deepened. "Don't tell me. . .you dug up more bones."

His attitude set Luke's teeth on edge. "You're about as funny as a bad accident, Rafferty."

Casey gripped his arm. He clamped his mouth shut. They had agreed not to mention his mother's accident until they'd wrapped up this more pressing business. He nodded, and she stepped forward.

"No more bones, Detective, but we think we know who the ones we found belong to."

"Oh? This ought to be good." He motioned to the chairs in front of his desk. "Fill me in on your great deductive reasoning, Miss Alexander, especially since forensics has yet to figure it out."

Casey perched on the edge of a chair, but Luke remained standing, much too uptight to sit still.

"They belong to Jack Kerrigan."

Rafferty's Adam's apple bobbed once, twice, before he leaned over his desk, clasping his fingers together. "Everyone in this town has seen Jack Kerrigan walking around, holding actual conversations, me included."

The sarcasm dripping from Rafferty's tone grated on Luke's already-tender nerves. He sat next to Casey and held out his hand. "Give me those pictures, Casey." He turned his attention to Rafferty. "If you would have done the job twenty-four years ago that Casey did in two weeks, you might have discovered this yourself."

He laid the pictures down on the desk. "The skull was missing some teeth."

Rafferty sat back and propped his hands behind his head, his expression more than a little indulgent. "Yeah. What of it?"

Luke held up the picture of his dad with the toothless grin standing next to John. "My dad, *Jack*, needed a partial after knocking out some teeth playing baseball. His brother, John, still has all his teeth. The person who's been walking around town pretending to be my father is none other than John."

Rafferty leaned forward, a sneer on his face. "You

mean to tell me you can't tell your uncle from your father? Come on, Luke."

He almost crumpled the picture in his fist. "I was only four when all this happened, Rafferty."

Casey touched his arm with one hand and took the picture from him with the other. "I think we went about this the wrong way. Let's start from the beginning."

"Great idea." Rafferty propped his chin on his hand. "Let's hear this ridiculous story from the beginning."

Luke had known that facing Rafferty wouldn't be easy, but his superior attitude certainly didn't help matters. Thankfully, Casey seemed calm in the storm. She even sat back in the chair and looked relaxed as she started the tale. Taking her cue, he sent up a prayer for strength, patience, and wisdom. Then he listened.

"You see, Detective, in the course of our investigation of Aunt Liddy's death, Luke and I discovered many things that each seemed like separate incidents at first, until we kept digging."

"Like what?"

"Like," Luke said, jumping in, "when Casey was attacked at the park when she went back after the rock that fell out of Lydia's shoe."

Rafferty raised his eyebrows at Casey. "You never told me you were attacked."

"Uh—" She threw a warning glance at Luke. "I was there after dark. I had a feeling I'd already riled you enough." Her fingers tightened on his arm. "But now I think it had to be John who attacked me. I bet he wanted the stones back."

"What stones?" Rafferty's brows puckered.

"Okay, let's try this again." Casey scooted to the edge

of her chair. "About twenty-three or twenty-four years ago, John Kerrigan somehow managed to steal raw gemstones being transported from Africa. Jack found out and paid to see the manifests so he could steal them from John. When John found out about it, the brothers got into a fight, and Jack ended up dead."

Rafferty looked skeptical. "So you're saying that John killed Jack and assumed his identity."

"Yes."

"And you think John buried his brother in Lydia's garden?"

Casey fidgeted. "From the letters I found in the attic, John and Aunt Liddy were in love. I think they worked together to bury the body."

"And you're basing all of this on an old picture of a toothless kid and a skull with missing teeth that could have fallen out just because of sheer age?"

Luke stood and pulled the partial from his pocket. "And this. I got it from Mrs. Teaser, who used to clean my dad's house. She said she found it while working there one day."

Rafferty sat back and rested his elbows on the armrests of his chair, his steepled fingers against his lips. "Okay. Very compelling. But what about the gemstones? If John found out about the theft, he should have been able to get the stones back. Have you uncovered any evidence that he still has them?"

Casey reached into her bag, pulled out the leather pouch, and opened it. "We found these in Aunt Liddy's attic. I'm assuming she got them from John."

Rafferty's eyes rounded as he leaned forward and took one of the stones. He held it up to the light and turned it in his fingers. "This is a gemstone?"

"A raw one. Uncut." She pulled out the book Monah had given her and opened it to the pictures. "Here's a good likeness of what you're holding."

Luke's cell phone rang. "Hello?"

"Luke, you gotta hurry. John just left his house with a suitcase, and now he's pulling up to the bank."

He flipped the phone shut. "John's running. He's at the bank."

Rafferty jumped from his chair and grabbed his suit coat. He headed for the door, shoving his arms into the sleeves, then turned back. "If you two have any thoughts of helping with this, forget them. We can handle this just fine. We've been catching criminals for years without your help. Just stay put."

Rafferty called for three other officers to join him and rushed out the front door. Luke turned to Casey. Her eyes were huge, her body stiff, as though ready to bolt. Same condition he was in. He motioned with his head. She nodded. They leaped from their chairs and ran for his truck.

Luke stomped on the gas. John was running. That made him guilty. No way would he miss this arrest.

The light turned red. He slowed, mumbling about his bad luck.

Casey clutched the dash. "What are you doing?"

"It's red."

She waved at the light. "But we're in hot pursuit. Besides, you can turn right on red. Go."

He glanced at her, checked for traffic, then made a hard right. "Hot pursuit? You watch too much television."

"I do not. I just read a lot, and that's what Brandy calls it."

They were almost to the patrol car. "Who's Brandy?"

"Oh, look." She patted his shoulder with one hand and pointed out the windshield with the other. "There they are."

"They?"

Monah stood in front of John on the bank's steps. He dwarfed her tiny body, but she stood her ground, her hands pressed to her hips and her shoulders squared.

He thumped the steering wheel. "She was supposed to stay in her car."

The words barely left his lips before he saw John look up. He shoved Monah out of the way, but she grabbed his arm and spun, ending up behind him. A quick kick to the back of the legs sent him to his knees. Monah pushed him to his belly, hopped on his back, and sat straddling him, still twisting his arm.

His jaw dropped. "What does she think she's doing?"

Casey bounced on the seat and slapped his leg repeatedly. "Did you see that? That's so cool."

"Cool?"

"Look out, Luke!"

He slammed on his brakes and cranked the steering wheel, just missing a police cruiser by inches. Gravel sprayed from the tires as he ground to a halt. They jumped out of the truck and darted toward Monah.

Rafferty dragged John to his feet. One of his men placed cuffs on John's wrists. Monah stood off to the side, her hands shoved into her pockets. Her hair was tousled, and her glasses lay on the ground.

The pounding of Luke's heart slowed. "Wait till I get ahold of her."

"I can't wait to talk to her, either. I didn't know she knew martial arts."

Casey's eyes were wide, and the faintest smile pulled at her lips. Ready with a retort about the danger, Luke clamped his mouth shut when the officers approached with his uncle in tow. Head down, John refused to look at him. Was he sorry? Did he even feel remorse?

Fingers curling into fists, Luke headed toward his uncle. Casey touched his arm. He jerked away. A roar like rushing water raged in his ears. Only yards from reaching John, Rafferty stepped between them.

"That's far enough, Luke."

He continued walking, pushing at Rafferty's chest, never taking his eyes from John. Rafferty grabbed him in a bear hug, swung him around, then held him at arm's length.

Rafferty shook his head. "Now's not the time. You

should have stayed at the station like I said. It would have been less emotional for you."

Casey moved beside Luke and wrapped her arms around him. He latched onto her like a lifeline, his jumbled emotions and heavy breathing slowing to normal as the police cars drove away.

A shudder went through him as the taillights disappeared around the corner. "I think that's the closest I've come to hating someone."

She looked up into his face. "You don't hate him, Luke."

He took another deep breath. "I did for a minute." Movement caught his attention. Monah stood at her car waving. He motioned her over, but she didn't move except to cup her hands to her mouth.

Her voice drifted toward them. "I'll meet you at the station."

He took Casey's hand and led her toward his truck. "Yeah, and then I'm going to have her locked up. What she did was crazy."

"Or brave."

He tossed her a scowl as she got in. She merely smirked at him.

In minutes they were back at police headquarters. They caught up to Monah and trailed her inside, Luke scolding all the way. "What were you thinking? You weren't supposed to confront John. Only keep an eye on him."

"I didn't confront him. I stalled him long enough for the police to arrive."

"You consider knocking him to the ground and sitting on his back stalling?"

She shrugged and smiled. "It worked, didn't it?"

Women! "You and Casey. It's like you think you're indestructible. I know how to stop Casey from going off on her own. I'll just take away her Post-its. She's helpless without them." That earned him a swat on the arm. "You, on the other hand—I guess I'll just have to swipe your glasses."

"Don't you dare. You know I can't see beans without them."

"Exactly."

He turned his attention to the commotion at the police counter. An officer rolled his uncle's fingers across an ink pad and pressed them onto some paper. Luke focused on the black circles. A part of him withered inside.

"He really planned to run, huh?"

The officer handed John a paper towel and led him into Rafferty's office. John flung one last look in Luke's direction before the door closed behind him. Luke couldn't read the look, but it hit him right in the heart.

"Appears that way." Monah's sympathetic expression matched the hug she gave him. "I'm sorry, Luke."

He nodded. Casey touched his arm.

"Why don't we all have a seat while we wait? Anyone want some coffee?"

Monah held up her hand. "I'll scrounge some up. I've been curious about what police station coffee tastes like anyway." She made a face. "No time like the present."

Rafferty's office door opened. "Luke." He waved him over. "Your uncle says he'll make a full confession, but only if you're in the room."

Your uncle.

Grief squeezed Luke's chest. He glanced over the detective's shoulder to see John's head hanging low.

"Casey's lost just as much as I have in this whole thing. She should join us."

Rafferty looked from him to Casey and back, his face reddening. "John never asked for her."

"That's the deal—take it or leave it."

After one last stare-down, Rafferty nodded. "Why should you start listening to me now?" He heaved a sigh. "All right. Get her in here. I'll explain to John." He pointed to the officer standing at the door. "Grab a couple more chairs. It seems this case is turning into a party."

Luke shrugged off the last phrase and motioned for Casey. "John won't talk without me in there. Want to join us?"

She cast a glance inside and took a step, her eyes hopeful. Then she stopped. "Should I? I mean—"

"I already told them you were." He put his arm around her shoulders. "Come on."

John hunched in a wooden chair beside Rafferty's large desk, his cuffed wrists in his lap. Light from the fluorescent bulbs overhead made him look pale, almost sickly.

They sat at an angle from John, who had yet to raise his head. The ache to wrap his arms around his uncle and tell him everything would be okay warred with the desire to give him a fist to the face. Luke did neither but remained silent and waited for the moment he could look his uncle in the eyes.

Rafferty flopped into his chair and planted his elbows on his desk. "All right, John. He's here. Start talking."

John's head lifted in slow increments, as though the action took great effort. Luke swallowed hard at the change in his uncle. His face had aged several years. Hair in disarray, wrinkled shirt, and red-rimmed eyes added to the deteriorated look. His expression begged. . .what? Forgiveness? Understanding?

Only one word came to mind. "Why?"

John's throat worked as he licked his dry lips. "It was an accident. I never meant for your dad to die. It's just—" He shook his head. His eyes took on a vacant look, as though he'd gone back twenty-four years.

Luke had to know what happened. "Just what?"

John blew out a long breath. "You were too young to remember. There was always so much competition between Jack and me. We never outgrew it. But Jack was a better businessman. Everything he touched made a profit. I was desperate to show him I could be just as good, so I tried to make money an easier way. I borrowed money from him using my trust fund as collateral. I figured there was no risk. The deal had already been made to"—he looked at Rafferty—"to steal the raw gemstones. All I needed was front money."

"And Dad provided it?"

"Yes. Seemed glad to help me out. I figured it just made him feel superior that I had to come to him for help." He squirmed in the chair. "I don't know how, but he found out about the shipment and got to it before me. I demanded to see the manifest when they told me the package had already been picked up. The signature showed only J. Kerrigan. Jack had beaten me again. Not only did he have the gems, but since I couldn't use them to pay him back, he'd also have my trust fund."

Rafferty sat back in his chair. "So you killed him."

John turned to him. "I told you. It was an accident." He closed his eyes and tipped his head back. "I went to his house in a rage. He didn't even try to explain. Just had this smirk on his face." His fists clenched.

Luke's heart picked up momentum. "You fought?"

"Yeah." John's head went back down, and he stared at his hands. "I guess my anger gave me the edge. The fight didn't last long. Only four or five hits, I guess. The last one sent him tumbling against the fireplace. His head hit the brick, and he never got back up." He looked up. "Luke, I swear I never meant to kill him."

A deep ache speared Luke's chest. "Why didn't you just go to the police if it was an accident?"

John slumped then turned to Casey. "Lydia asked me the same thing when I called her. I told her what happened when I got there and convinced her that if the police knew, I'd be tried not only as a murderer, but also as a thief."

Tears trickled along Casey's nose. She pulled a packet of tissues from her bag. "So she helped you hide the body in her garden."

"Yes. I hate that I involved her. I should have just dealt with it myself." He shifted in his chair, making the handcuffs rattle. "She's always been there for me. My cheerleader, encourager, and soul mate. I think it was instinct to pick up the phone and call her. She never even flinched when I asked for her help—her love for me was that deep."

"And you used that love." Casey's voice broke.

Silence stretched for several moments. John cleared his throat. "Can I ask, um, well. . .how did you find Jack's body?"

Casey wiped at her nose again. "Her roses died." She took a deep, trembling breath. "Where is she, John? Where'd you hide her body?"

His head whipped up. "What?" He tried to stand. The officer behind him slammed him back into the chair. He shrugged away from the officer's hand. "I didn't kill her, Casey. I give you my word. I have no idea where she is. I looked just as hard for her as you did."

"I don't believe that."

"It's true. I admit, I offered to buy the house and even tried to run you off the road and messed with your brake line to keep you from discovering Jack's body, but I just wanted to scare you away. I never meant to hurt you."

"That was you in Maxwell's truck?"

His chin fell to his chest. "Yes. I'm sorry."

Luke wasn't sure whether to trust the sincerity in John's voice. He'd managed to deceive everyone for so long, his acting skills were well honed. A glance at Casey's squinted eyes told him she felt the same way. He decided to take the lead.

"We think you killed Lydia because she wanted to confess."

John shook his head.

Luke plowed ahead. "She must have been afraid of that very thing, so she sent Casey a letter with the key, just in case the worst happened."

"No."

"The only way you could keep her from telling the police and continue protecting yourself was to kill her, too."

"No." His voice cracked as his eyes pooled. "She did want to confess. She said what she'd done ate at her once she was saved." He took a gasping breath. "But I couldn't hurt her. Not for anything. I'd die first."

Luke wavered in his belief. His uncle sounded so genuine.

Rafferty leaned across his desk. "I'm guessing you acquired the stolen gemstones at the same time you assumed your brother's identity. Where are they? How many were there? Did you sell them?"

John wilted in the seat. "No, not all of them were sold. Not right away, anyway." His voice rasped like that of an old man. "I gave some to Lydia in case she ever needed money."

"How many?"

"Hmm?"

Rafferty scowled. "How many did you give her?"

"Four. I sold the rest piecemeal over the years. One or two at a time."

Picking up the leather pouch Casey had given him earlier, Rafferty shook out the stones and looked at her. "There's only three in here."

"We told you, one was taken from me at the park."

"Oh, right. And you thought John attacked you to get it back."

John sat up straight. "I never attacked Casey." He turned to her. "I never attacked you."

Rafferty waved his hand. "We'll get to that later. What was the total number of stolen rocks?" He grabbed up the gemstone book Casey had left on his desk and flipped to her marker.

"Twenty-four."

"Liar." He turned the page toward John. "This book says thirty."

John took a breath as though he was completely worn out. "No, there were only twenty-four gemstones in the box. If more are missing, I don't know where they are."

The book slid from Rafferty's grasp onto his desk. He

sat back in his chair, his hand going up to his mouth as he stared at John. Then he turned to Casey. "So if he doesn't have the rest of the stones, where'd they go?"

Casey squeezed Luke's hand. Luke shifted forward in his seat. "Detective Rafferty—"

"Thanks for your help." She shot to her feet and dragged him with her. "But I think it's time we got going."

He looked down at her in amazement. She stared back, eyes pleading, and suddenly, he understood. Richard was her father. If she wanted to talk to him first, he'd let her. But he had no intention of letting her go alone.

A wave of nausea swept over Casey, but she made herself reach for the door handle.

"Are you sure you want to do this? It'd be easier to just tell Rafferty what you know."

She glanced over her shoulder at Luke. He looked so sweet in his T-shirt and jeans—how could she have thought him a murderer? "It may be easier, but it wouldn't be right."

He touched her cheek, his fingers warm upon her skin. "If you want me to tell him—"

She shook her head. "I can do it. I want to. I'm almost hoping he volunteers to tell the police what he knows. Maybe then I'll finally believe all the stuff he's told me the last couple of days."

She got out of the truck and waited on the sidewalk while Luke rounded to join her. Up ahead, a cheerful sign painted ivory and green announced MABEL'S BED & BREAKFAST. She moved toward it.

"He said he'd be waiting in the foyer. Do you think he will? Maybe he's figured out why we've come, and left town so he can protect his reputation."

But Richard waited by the stairs, his hair neatly combed and his black polo shirt tucked into his khakis.

He moved toward them, arms opened wide. "I'm so glad you called. I'd hoped, but not until I heard your voice did I actually think—"

Casey held up her hand to stop him. "This isn't a social visit, Dad. We need to talk."

A broad smile stretched across his face. "Dad?"

Her heart dropped to her toes. Why had that slipped out? She tore her gaze away from his pleased grin. "Is there someplace quiet we can go?"

He gestured toward a small parlor off the hall. "In here." The pocket doors swooshed as he slid them closed. He joined her on the settee. "Is this about Liddy?"

She twisted her fingers in her lap. "In a way." Luke's steady gaze bolstered her courage. "You remember when you said you'd do whatever I needed you to do?"

Richard stiffened as if he knew the question trembling on her lips. He crossed his arms. "Yeah."

"Well, there is something. . .that is. . .we talked to Rafferty, and. . ." Tears welled in her eyes, and her hands trembled. She stared at her father in mute silence. To her amazement, dampness sprang to his eyes, as well, and his shoulders slumped.

"Looks like this may not be quite the happy ending I'd envisioned."

"Dad—"

"What is it they want me to do? Testify against John?"

She nodded, glad when Luke rose and placed his hands on her shoulders. "They will, once they find out what you know. We didn't tell them."

Richard got up and walked to the window, his hands jammed into the pockets of his slacks. "They arrested him."

She forced back the knot constricting her throat. "Yes."

Laughter floated from the hallway. More guests. She should have figured he wouldn't be the only one registered.

Richard waited while the house quieted. "When did they pick him up?"

She hated to say it, and yet a part of her yearned to know if he'd follow through. "About an hour ago."

He turned at her whispered reply. She expected lines of stress, perhaps a worried frown. Instead, he looked peaceful—or was it resigned?

"Do I have time to get my coat?"

Her heart jumped. She stood. "You're coming now?"

He approached her but made no move to touch her as he did before. "I made you a promise, Case, the first one in years. I intend to keep it."

Tears streamed down her face like a burst dam. "The statute of limitations on your crime probably expired a long time ago. If you choose, you can walk away, and no one will ever know what you did."

Sadness clouded Richard's gaze. He lifted his chin. "You could never be okay with that. I'll do the right thing, Casey. I figure it's about time."

Casey crossed the distance between them in two quick steps. And when she wrapped her arms around his waist, a part of her deep inside danced.

Luke leaned over to shake Richard's hand, impressed with the way he'd laid out the details to Rafferty with very little apprehension. The fact that he did it for his daughter left an imprint Luke would not soon forget.

Rafferty stood. "Well, Mr. Alexander, it seems all that's left is to get your official statement." He clapped him on the back. "Come on. I'll walk you through the process."

"Dad?" Casey jumped from her chair and ran to him.

The two embraced for several moments, accompanied

by mumbles and sniffles. She leaned against the doorjamb of Rafferty's office as Rafferty led him away. Luke moved behind her and touched her shoulder. She spun into his arms and pressed her face against his chest. He held her until her sobs subsided.

"Let's sit for a while. I don't think there's any hurry to leave, is there?"

She shook her head. They chose the chairs closest to Rafferty's desk. Except for phones ringing and the chatter from the officers drifting in, the room was quiet. Luke would sit and hold her hand until she felt ready to talk.

Papers and folders littered Rafferty's desk. How on earth did the man keep anything straight? One folder caught Luke's attention, the tab sporting the name KERRIGAN. The detective certainly didn't lag in cases if he already had one for his dad—*uncle*. The transition would take awhile to register in his mind.

A large manila envelope below his uncle's file lay at an angle with most of the return address hidden—ENSICS LABORATORIES.

He leaned forward and bumped John's file over, revealing the logo of the Massachusetts State Forensics Laboratories. His heart clanged a crazy rhythm.

"Didn't Rafferty say he hadn't received the results from the bones?"

"What?"

He turned to Casey. "I thought Rafferty said earlier he was still waiting for the forensic evidence."

"He did."

He glanced at the door and pulled the envelope onto his lap. "Then what's this?" He slipped a folder out of the envelope, flipped it open, and read the first line. "This is it. The evidence we've been waiting for. I wonder why Rafferty didn't say anything."

"Maybe it came in while we were at my dad's."

"Maybe." He skimmed the pages. One line kept him from reading farther. "Go watch for Rafferty."

"Luke—"

"Hurry, Case. If he's headed this way, stall him."

"What?"

He looked her dead in the eyes. "Don't let him in here."

She returned to the door, leaning just as before. He stood, set the folder on the desk, and pulled out his cell phone. Page by page he took pictures, storing them until he could read the entire report later.

"Detective." Casey's voice flowed through the door. "How's my dad?"

He continued snapping the pictures, hoping his haste didn't make them blur.

"He's fine. Just giving his statement to a clerk."

"You're taking good care of him, right?"

"Of course."

The voices sounded closer. *I need more time.*

"I mean, he did confess on his own. That ought to earn him some privileges."

"Miss Alexander, we treat everyone well, no matter who they are or what they've done."

Footsteps clomped a little louder on the tiles. Only two more pages left.

"Detective."

"Look, Miss Alexander. . ."

The footsteps stopped. He kept clicking.

"I have nothing but respect for your father. What he

did is nothing short of amazing. He'll be treated well. You have my word."

Luke slapped the folder closed, pushed it back in the envelope, placed it under John's file, then tried to look as casual in his chair as possible.

Rafferty shoved through the door. His eyes narrowed when he spotted Luke. "What are you still doing in here?"

He stood and moved to Casey's side. "Just waiting on her." He put his arm around her shoulders. "I see you found him. Did you get all your questions asked?" She nodded. "Good." He turned to Rafferty. "Are we finished here, or do we need to make a statement or something?"

"The interviews were recorded. That's enough for now." He waved them away as he rounded his desk. "I know where to find you if I need more."

"Great." He propelled Casey out the door. "Thanks for all your help, Detective," he called over his shoulder.

Once inside the pickup, Casey spun toward him. "What was that all about?"

He turned the key, backed out of the lot, then gunned the engine toward Lydia's.

"Luke, what was in that report?"

He relaxed his clenched jaw, still struggling with disbelief. "Dad didn't die from a blow to the head."

Casey blinked and shook her head. Surely she didn't hear that right. "What did you say?"

Luke's chest rose and fell in quick jerks. "The report listed trauma to the jaw and skull as injuries, but under cause of death, it said some kind of poisoning." He waved his hand. "I didn't get a good look at it because I was in such a rush. Have you got a computer handy where we can transfer these pictures?"

One eyebrow lifted. "Are you kidding? I'm a Web designer. Just get me back to Aunt Lydia's. We can look more closely there."

She jumped from the vehicle the moment it rolled to a stop and darted up the steps. Excitement shook her hands, and it took several tries for her to get the key in the door. Finally, it sprang open, and Casey hurried upstairs to fetch her laptop. She deposited it on the kitchen table and gave Luke her address while she turned it on. The moments while it booted dragged by.

She plugged in her wireless card and hit the CONNECT tab. "Have you e-mailed them?"

Luke's fingers flew over the number pad on his cell phone. "You should be getting them now."

They hunched over the keyboard, eyes trained on the progress bar while the pictures were received.

"Done!"

She jumped at Luke's sharp exclamation. "Jinkies, you scared me."

He rubbed her shoulder. "Sorry. I'll try to keep it

down. Right there." He pointed at the screen. Open that one first."

She sat down to work, enlarging the image and adjusting the contrast to make it easier to read. "What are we looking for again?"

"Copper something. That's not it. Go to the next page."

She closed the file and opened the next one.

"That one. Scroll down."

She sped past the medical mumbo-jumbo, pausing on a line that listed the missing teeth as an injury older than the one to the head.

"The baseball accident when he was a kid."

Luke nodded. "Yeah. Keep going."

"'Young male, average height and build,'" Casey read aloud. "Here it is. 'Cause of death: chromated copper arsenate poisoning.' What is *that*?"

"That's. . . If I'm not mistaken, that's. . ." Luke straightened and scratched his head. "Arsenic."

"Hold on a minute." Casey opened a search engine, typed in the words, and hit ENTER. The results were almost instantaneous. Listed among them was Wikipedia.

Luke jammed his finger at the screen. "Try that one."

By the rasp in his voice, Casey knew he was as nervous and excited as she was. She clicked on the link, leaning closer to the screen as the page opened. Beside her, Luke did the same.

She skimmed through the paragraph citing the composition and atomic weight of the element, coming at last to a line that confirmed Luke's idea. She pointed. "You're right. It's arsenic, or at least, part of it is."

"What does it say?"

She scrolled farther down. "Okay, wait. . .right here. Read this."

"'The application of most concern to the general public is probably that of wood which has been treated with chromated copper arsenate.'"

He slapped his forehead. "CCA. I've got a pile of that wood stacked behind the nursery. I never knew what to do with it, but I didn't want to use it because of the health hazard."

Her hand fluttered through the air. "Keep reading."

He leaned forward. "'CCA timber is still in widespread use in many countries and was heavily used during the latter half of the twentieth century as a structural and outdoor building material, where there was a risk of rot or insect infestation in untreated timber.'" He paused and skimmed the page with his finger then resumed reading. "'Recent years have seen fatal animal poisonings and serious human poisonings resulting from the ingestion—directly or indirectly—of wood ash from CCA timber (the lethal human dose is approximately 20 grams of ash).'"

They fell silent. Casey struggled to process what Luke had just read. "So let me make sure I understand. They used to treat wood with arsenic?"

Luke dropped into the chair next to her. "Uh-huh. Did you catch the part about the ashes being lethal?"

"Yes. Twenty grams—that's not very much, is it?"

"About a tablespoon."

Her mouth dropped open. "That's all it takes to kill a person? How available is this stuff?"

"Like I said, I have a pile of wood treated with it at the nursery."

A knot formed in her stomach. She clutched Luke's

arm. "Oh, Luke. What about John? He said he killed Jack by accident. Did he know about the poison?"

"How could he, unless he did it?"

"But why would he lie about how he killed him?"

"Maybe he figured he'd get a lighter sentence if he said it was an accident."

She thought about that for a second and then shook her head. "I don't think so. I think he really believes Jack died in the fight."

They stared at each other in silence. Casey's hand inched toward the Post-its in her purse. "Let's suppose John only thought he killed Jack. Let's suppose someone else poisoned him and then let John think he did it when the two of them fought."

A bit of color drained from Luke's tanned face. "Okay."

Casey paused in reaching for a pencil to rub the goose bumps from her flesh. "And suppose the report didn't arrive on Rafferty's desk when I went to my dad's. I mean, the mail usually runs early, doesn't it? Like in the morning? So suppose it got there earlier and Rafferty knew what it said and hid it, hoping we wouldn't see it."

The hum of the refrigerator filled the quiet kitchen.

Luke's green eyes darkened. "That's a lot of supposing."

Casey tapped her temple, thinking. "The envelope was open when you looked at the report, so he had to have read it. Even if I'm wrong about when he got it, why wouldn't he have told us when we went back? Why did he arrest John for murder, knowing full well it wasn't trauma to the head that killed Jack?"

After a long pause, Luke shook his head. "I don't know."

She slapped the table. "The money."

"Huh?"

"Carol's package. Remember when I told you Carol handed Rafferty a bag at the rest area?"

"Yeah." His eyebrows shot up. "You think Rafferty was blackmailing Carol?"

She grasped a lock of her hair and wound it around her index finger. "Maybe. We figured the two cases were unrelated, but what if they're not? What if Carol poisoned Jack, then let John think he killed him in a fight? Somehow, Rafferty could have found out about it and started blackmailing her for the money he needed to keep his wife in a home."

Luke gave a slow nod. "Or vice versa."

"What?"

"You may have been right the first time. Carol may have been paying Rafferty off for helping her get out of the embezzling trouble. In which case, Rafferty could be the one who did the poisoning and hid the report to cover his own tracks."

"Either way, they were both involved."

Luke nodded in agreement. "I think so."

"So then, we need to corner them both."

He grabbed her arm. "Don't even suggest that I let you go after Carol alone."

She grinned, warmed by his concern. "I was going to suggest we call Mike Brockman." She pulled a white business card from a pocket of her purse. "He gave me this when I first came to town. If he picks up Carol, we can all go back to the station together and finally get this thing resolved."

He slid his cell phone across the table to her. "Do it."

She dialed the number. Brockman answered on the second ring. After cautioning him to be discreet, Casey related everything she and Luke had learned, glancing at him as she finished to be sure she hadn't left anything out. Finally, she flipped the phone closed.

"What'd he say?"

"He said he'd pick up Carol and meet us here."

"Did he say how long?"

A knock sounded on the front door.

Foreboding raised the hairs on Casey's neck. She froze and turned wide eyes to Luke, who remained rooted to his seat, the same as she. For several seconds neither one moved. Finally, she stood, walked to the living room window, and pulled back the curtain to look.

25

The chair scraped back as Luke rose from the table. "Who is it?"

Casey pressed closer to the glass. The front porch was empty, but the lights were on, tripped by the motion sensor even in daylight. "I don't know. I can't see anybody." She reached for the handle and gave it a turn.

"Don't open that!" Luke flew down the hall and knocked her hand away. "Get away from the window!"

"What?"

He pushed her against the wall and leaned close, his body covering hers. Fear made her heart hurry. "What's the matter?"

"I don't know. I just have this feeling—"

Something smashed against the back door. She screamed and buried her face in his shoulder. He grabbed her and threw her to the floor a moment before a second kick burst the door open.

"Stay here," he mouthed.

She clutched his arm and shook her head. He squeezed her fingers and pushed to his feet.

"Luke? Casey? Come out. I need to speak to you."

Rafferty! Casey's eyes widened. She stared at Luke in silent appeal. He gestured, palm out, for her to stay hidden.

"There's an emergency down at the station, a problem with your father. Must've been the stress. He needs you, Casey. He's asking for you." His voice drew closer with every word.

Luke inched around the hall tree and darted into the den. Casey scrambled to her knees and scurried behind the couch. An afghan lay draped over the back. She pulled it over her head.

"I called for the paramedics before I came. I tried to call you, but there was no answer. Your cell phone must be off, and Luke's was busy." His footsteps hit the hardwood floor of the hallway.

Desperate, and scared out of her wits for Luke's safety, she started to pray.

"C'mon now, guys. There's no need for this. I know you're here. I saw the truck outside."

She blew out a breath, trying to regulate the action of her lungs and the pounding of her heart by sheer strength of will.

"Case—"

He was in the room! Her insides shrieked for her to run. She squeezed her eyes shut. Maybe if she couldn't see him. . .

"I see you."

"No!" Luke's hoarse yell shattered the silence following Rafferty's deadly whisper. She heard scuffling, followed by a loud crash.

"Casey, run!"

She jerked out from under the blanket. In the middle of the room, Luke and Rafferty struggled over a gun.

"Run!"

She ran.

Their bodies blocked the way to the entrance. She hurdled the chair beside them. Her knee struck the back. It landed with a thud on the floor. "Luke!"

"No." Rafferty snarled and lunged toward her, throwing

both him and Luke onto the carpet.

Luke grunted. Rafferty clawed for the lamp on the end table. She couldn't snatch it away. He grabbed it and brought it smashing down on Luke's head. She screamed.

Dazed, Luke lost his grip on Rafferty's gun. Rafferty ripped free and bolted to his feet.

"Don't move, either of you." He wiped a bit of blood from his lip where Luke had hit him. "Get up." He kicked Luke and gestured to Casey with the gun. "Come here."

She hesitated.

"Now, or I kill him!"

"Okay!" Her hands shook as she pleaded with him. "Don't shoot him."

The crazed look in Rafferty's eyes faded as she moved closer.

"No," Luke groaned. "Casey, don't—"

"Shut up," Rafferty shouted, pointing his pistol at Luke's head. He looked immense blocking the doorway, the light from the hall shrouding his face in shadow. He grabbed Casey's arm and jerked her to his side, his steely fingers pinching bruises on her flesh. "You had to do it, didn't you? You had to come meddling where you didn't belong."

Tears streamed down her face. "I had to find Aunt Liddy."

He roared with rage. "Auntie Liddy. That's all I've heard from you. I'm sick of it!" He squeezed tighter.

"Why did you do it? Why did you kill her? Did she find out about your secret? How you poisoned Jack and then let John think he killed him?"

An evil grin spread across Rafferty's face. "You think you're smart, eh? Not clever enough to put the envelope containing the forensics report back where I left it." He brought his face closer, his stale-coffee-tainted breath making her stomach lurch. "Not smart enough to figure out that it was me who attacked you in the park, not John." He leaned back with a smile and held up the leather pouch containing the gemstones. "I didn't kill your aunt, but thanks to you and your snooping, I've got enough money to start a brand-new life."

Trembling seized her. "If you didn't kill her, who did?"

Rafferty cocked the pistol and brought it to her temple. "You'll know soon enough."

A scream pierced the air. For a moment, confusion paralyzed Rafferty. Casey jerked away just as something—a garden hoe?—came crashing down on his arm. The gun skittered into the hallway. From his knees, Luke threw himself into Rafferty's legs and dropped him to the floor. In a matter of seconds, he sat on top of him, Rafferty's arm pinned behind his back.

"Are you okay? Casey! Is everyone all right?"

Casey blinked in terror. She couldn't breathe, could barely think. "Yes. I'm fine," she gasped. "Who—?"

They turned their eyes to the black-clad, hoe-wielding form standing in the entrance to the room. Whoever it was puffed for air, blowing the face-covering veil up and out until it slid from the pins holding it and settled slightly askew.

Shock rolled through Casey's body. Her knees gave way. She fumbled for something to grab on to and found the edge of the couch. She stared, mouth dry, at the person peering back. Afraid to move, or even blink, she sucked in a breath and forced herself to speak.

"Aunt Liddy?"

With shaking fingers, Lydia tugged the veil the rest of the way off. Her white hair gleamed against the black blouse she wore, and a crooked grin tipped her lips. "Hello, Casey." Aunt Liddy picked up the gun then crossed to stand next to her. She gestured to Luke. "It's okay, Luke. You can get up. I've got him. Use the cord from the lamp to tie his hands."

He hesitated, the look in his eyes reflecting the disbelief that Casey felt. "Lydia?" He bound Rafferty's hands then shoved him away and rose to his feet. "You're alive?"

The gun trained on Rafferty, Lydia nodded. "I hated having to do this to you both, but there was no other way, and I was desperate." Tears spilled down her cheeks. She wiped them away with the back of her hand.

Bombarded by emotion, Casey struggled to form a sentence. "But—where have you been?"

"Hiding out with Ethel Dunn."

"Who?"

"The lady you met at the post office."

Casey thought hard. "The one asking all the questions when I first got to town."

"That's her. She and I planned this elaborate scheme to get Rafferty to uncover the person behind the threats."

"I'm confused." Casey stopped her with a wave of her hand. "What threats?"

Aunt Liddy drew a deep breath. "It all started several months ago, after Monah led me to Christ. I found notes taped to my door."

"What'd they say?"

"Warnings about coming clean, things like that. I guess being vocal about my salvation made Rafferty nervous. Made him think I'd be tempted to confess what I knew. Of course, I didn't know it was him back then."

"So the notes made you realize there was more going on than you thought."

"Exactly. You see, all these years, I thought John killed Jack. It wasn't until the threats started that I figured out someone else was involved. I had to find out who, especially if it meant we'd been wrong, and John was innocent of the crime. I planted clues, thinking they would draw the real killer out."

"The suicide note, the stone in the shoe, the key to the wooden chest where we found the stones, the shoe box filled with photographs, the letters in the attic, the dead roses." Casey went back through her mental list, ticking them off one by one. "That was all you?"

Aunt Liddy nodded. "Except for the key. That was my backup plan. I thought if the worst happened, if my plan failed and the killer got me before I could discover his identity, the key might lead you to uncover the truth."

"But I. . .I don't understand." Confusion shook Casey's insides.

"I never dreamed all of this would put you in danger. You were so busy with your new Web design business. I thought we'd have the case solved before you got wind of my suicide. I knew faking my death was wrong, but there was no other way."

A growl rumbled from Rafferty's throat. "I knew I shouldn't have bothered with the notes. I should have killed you and been done with it."

Aunt Liddy raised the gun. "Be quiet. I'm through being afraid of you."

"So then what?" Luke interrupted. "Casey showed up?"

"Yes." Aunt Liddy turned her gaze back. "Knowing the plan had been to turn myself in once the person behind the threats was uncovered, Ethel was a bit rattled to see you in Pine Mills. She raced back to tell me you were in town. I almost went to the police right then, Casey, but Ethel convinced me our plan could still work." She plucked at the dark clothing. "I never intended on skulking around the park, my own memorial service, and home looking like something out of a comic book. I had to come up with a way to stay close enough to protect you but not let myself be recognized. We thought if the police believed I was really dead, they would have to investigate."

A chill ran up Casey's arms. She rubbed it away with both hands. "Did John know about the threats and your plan?"

A vehement shake ruffled Aunt Liddy's curls. "No. I figured if I left him out of it, the killer would only be after me." Her gaze softened. "I'm so sorry, darling. I would never have had the heart to go through with this if I thought it would put you in danger."

"Sorry, darling. Sorry, darling." Rafferty twisted against the cord binding his wrists. "If I ever get loose—"

Casey and Aunt Liddy turned in unison. "Be quiet."

Luke nudged Rafferty with his toe. "You'd better hope you don't. I'd love a reason to pummel you."

Rafferty fell silent.

"You were saying," Casey said.

"Jack was always a good businessman. John, on the other hand, struggled. He lost the first half of his trust fund a year after he received it. The second half wouldn't be paid to him until his twenty-fourth birthday. Desperate for money, he went to Jack and asked for a loan."

"The start of their disagreement?"

Lydia nodded. "Right. You see, Jack made John use the second half of his trust fund as collateral. Foolish as it was, John agreed. He wasn't worried about repaying the loan because of a shipment of uncut gemstones he was expecting the following month. Except that Jack found out about the shipment and stole them before John could get his hands on them."

"Richard."

"Yes, Richard." She sighed. "Jack wanted all of the money from the shipment *and* John's trust fund, and he used my brother to find out how he could take it. After the argument, John appeared on my doorstep, crazed with grief and ranting about an accident." Her blue eyes filled with tears. "I'm so sorry, Casey. I know it was wrong, but I agreed to help him. I loved him so much, I would have done anything he asked."

"Even bury my father without a word to anyone about what happened."

Luke's hoarse words froze them both. Disillusionment and pain darkened his eyes. Aunt Liddy took a step toward him. He put up his hand to stop her.

Aunt Liddy's shoulders slumped. "I've wronged you as much as I've wronged Casey. I couldn't stand keeping the truth from you any longer, Luke. You were like a son to me after your mother died."

His gaze sharpened. "Did you know about that? Did you know about Rafferty's part in her death? Or that he poisoned my dad?"

"You can't prove that. It's his word against mine." Rafferty struggled to sit.

"Be quiet!" All three turned to glare at him.

Finally, Aunt Liddy shook her head. "Poison? What's this about poison?"

Luke's face turned red. "The examiner's report stated that Dad died from arsenic poisoning, not a blow to the head."

Aunt Liddy reached for him again then let her hands fall to her sides. "No. I never knew of his involvement in your mother's death or that he poisoned Jack. All these years, we thought John did it."

"But none of this makes any sense," Casey said. "Why did Rafferty do it? Why kill Jack?"

"I know."

Carol Hester appeared at the door, Officer Brockman's tall form at her side.

Casey stood and directed a pointed stare at Carol. "What did you say?"

"I know why he did it, but I won't tell you unless"— she tilted her head to peer at Brockman—"unless you promise I won't go to jail."

Brockman led her farther into the house. "Your crimes aren't for me to decide, Ms. Hester, but assisting in this investigation is only going to help your cause. If you know something, I suggest you don't withhold it."

"Don't you dare," Rafferty growled. "Not one word out of you, do you hear me?" He glared at Brockman. "Neither of us is saying anything until we have a lawyer. Stupid as Carol is, she knows better."

Carol stiffened. "You know what? I'm sick of your threats." She whirled to Casey. "He did it. I saw him put the ashes in Jack's food."

"Shut up!"

"No, you shut up! I won't be bound to you a second

longer!" Hysterics made her voice shrill. "I was young, stupid, like he said." Her finger shook as she pointed at Rafferty. "He found out I had embezzled some money from my job and offered to help me get off in exchange for a favor. I didn't know I'd be tied to him for the next twenty-four years."

She looked about to break. Casey walked over to her and touched her shoulder. "Tell us why he did it, Carol."

She drew a shuddering breath. "Rafferty liked to gamble, but he wasn't very good at it. He lost a bunch of money and was in danger of losing his job. He went to Jack, who agreed to bail him out of his problems, but Rafferty had to consent to provide information and favors whenever Jack asked. Then when Rafferty's wife accidentally killed Mrs. Kerrigan. . ." Her voice trailed off to a whisper.

Casey took pity on her. "He got desperate and figured he'd get rid of his problem by poisoning Jack?"

"Yes."

"How did he know about the ashes?" Casey asked.

"A friend of his, the guy Luke bought his nursery from, told him. Rafferty made an appointment to meet Jack for dinner at some fancy Italian restaurant in Marlborough. I was supposed to distract Jack, keep him occupied for a few minutes." She directed an appealing glance at Brockman. "I didn't know he intended to put arsenic in the food until afterward."

"Arsenic? What'd I miss?" All heads swiveled to the door. A bewildered Monah looked from one to the other. "Well?"

Casey rushed to her. "Monah! We forgot all about you."

"Yeah, I know." Monah pushed her glasses farther

up her nose with her finger. "I went to get coffee, and when I got back, everybody was gone. So what's this about arsenic?"

"Rafferty used it to kill Jack."

"Rafferty!" Magnified by the lenses, Monah's bulging eyes nearly filled the frames. "Rafferty killed Jack?"

Luke nodded. "With ashes he got from burning pressure-treated lumber."

Monah tipped her head left, her finger tapping at her chin. "Riiight. Arsenic ashes. Fast-acting, if memory serves. Something like thirty minutes to a few hours depending on circumstances and the size of the person."

Brockman gaped at her. "Why do you know that?"

Monah spread her hands. "What? I read it in a book."

His bafflement evident, Brockman's lips parted as though to speak, but then he shook his head and motioned for Carol to continue.

"Where was I?"

"Rafferty poisoned Jack's food."

"Yeah. They finished eating, and then Jack left the restaurant. I never saw him alive again after that."

"No one did," Aunt Liddy said, stepping forward, "except John. That must have been when they fought, and when John thought he'd accidentally killed his brother."

Carol nodded. "John left town for a few weeks. When he got back, he claimed to be Jack. A few months later, he told everyone John was killed in a sailing accident. I knew better, but I also figured my trail would be covered if no one found out he was lying, so I kept my mouth shut." Her head lowered. "I was scared."

Casey squeezed her hand. "Rafferty must've thought he was the luckiest man alive when John and Aunt Liddy buried his problem for him in the garden."

Carol shuddered. "Yes."

Struck by an idea, Casey tapped her temple. "Carol, did Rafferty help you get a job at Kerrigan, Inc.?"

Carol looked up, her brows arched in surprise. "Yes. How did you know that?"

"And the bag I saw the two of you exchange at the rest area?"

Carol's gaze swung to Rafferty, who knelt with shoulders hunched, staring at the floor. "Money he made me steal from the company to help pay for his wife's hospital bills and his mounting gambling debts."

Casey folded her arms across her chest. "I thought so." She looked at Brockman. "So that's it, then? You have enough evidence to take him into custody?"

He nodded. "Sure do. I'll need everyone to come down to the station, including you, Ms. Lydia. I'm afraid I'm going to have to place you under arrest, even though I think the DA will be willing to work out a deal with you in exchange for your testimony and as a reward for your part in helping us uncover the missing pieces."

Aunt Liddy nodded.

"And, Luke, now that we know John isn't your father, you're probably going to want to get a lawyer to help you sort through the legal ramifications of acquiring your inheritance."

Luke agreed with a nod of his head. Casey crossed to him and slid her arm around his waist, thrilled by the feel of his arm pressing her close.

Within moments, Brockman had Rafferty in handcuffs and Carol in custody. She moped in the front seat of his squad car as he loaded Rafferty into the back. Using the radio, Brockman called for backup.

Casey was never so happy to wait. She took Luke's hand and led him back to the sofa where Aunt Liddy sat. Despite everything, Aunt Liddy and Luke still had a lot to work through, and she intended to help them get started.

Tears pooled in her eyes. Funny how she'd started out thinking all she wanted was to find her aunt's killer, when deep down, she realized it had been so much more. Trust. Security. Forgiveness. Now that she'd learned what she'd really wanted all along, she had no intention of letting it slip away.

She cast a glance heavenward, silently thanking God for watching over them. Maybe it wasn't a coincidence that she'd landed in Pine Mills. Maybe it had been His plan for her all along.

"Okay, God," she whispered, turning her back on Luke and Aunt Liddy to give them privacy as they talked. "You've been speaking to me about trust ever since I got here. All of this has shown me how important it is to be able to trust in something. So? What is it you want me to hear?" She pushed a strand of hair behind her ear and closed her eyes. "I'm listening."

26

The sun shone brightly on the final day of the trial. With her hand tucked into Luke's, Casey felt loved and secure, a sensation she was fast becoming accustomed to.

Inside the courthouse, Aunt Liddy and John awaited sentencing. They faced lesser charges than Rafferty and Carol, both of whom faced first-degree murder. Thanks to a plea bargain in exchange for her testimony, Aunt Liddy's lawyer appeared optimistic that she would serve no time, unlike John.

Richard faced no charges after all, since the statute of limitations on both the theft of the gemstones and the bribe he'd accepted to reveal the ship's manifest had long since expired.

"You ready?"

She glanced up at Luke. Amazing. His concern was for her alone. "Luke, wait." She tugged on his hand to keep him from going up the steps. "One last thing."

He paused, an adorable frown scrunching the skin between his eyebrows. "What's the matter?"

"Nothing. I just wanted you to know. . .I've decided to move my Web design business to Pine Mills permanently. I figured, whatever happens, I'll want to be near Aunt Liddy once this is all over, and maybe it'll help me and my dad get closer. Plus. . .I sort of hoped. . .you might be happy."

He grinned, the dimple she loved so much deepening on his cheek. He pressed a kiss to her lips. "I love you, you know that?"

Elation soared through her. "I love you, too."

"And I'm glad you're moving to Pine Mills."

She squinted up at him. "Why? So you don't have to commute back and forth to Virginia Beach?"

He shook his head and kissed the tip of her nose. "No, so you don't have to. I've seen the way you drive."

She laughed and smacked his arm.

"And, Casey?"

"Yeah?"

"Maybe by the time you're ready to go back for your things, your car will finally be finished."

She laughed outright, a picture of old Bob leaping to her memory. Somehow, she doubted that.

Elizabeth Ludwig graduated Summa Cum Laude from Hart High School in 1985. She received a scholarship to Michigan State University in 1986 and went on to study English and Journalism. She spent several years learning both music and theater arts and has performed in numerous community projects. She teaches a College and Career Sunday school class and sings on the praise team at her local church. She is an accomplished speaker and dramatist.

Mrs. Ludwig has written a number of historical books and two romantic suspense novels including *A Walk of Faith*, a finalist in ACFW's 2004 Noble Theme Contest. In 2005, Mrs. Ludwig was a finalist in two categories, General Historical and Historical Romance. She works full-time and lives with her husband and two children in Texas.

Janelle Mowery lives in Texas with her husband and two sons, though a portion of her heart still resides in her birth state of Minnesota. Janelle began writing inspirational stories in 2001 and has since written several historical novels. One of those novels won first place in the San Gabriel Writers' League "Writing Smarter" Contest in 2005. Two other novels were finalists in ACFW's Noble Theme Contest. When she isn't writing, her interests include reading and visiting historical sites, even if she can only get there by the Internet. To know more, visit her Web site at www.janellemowery.com.

You may correspond with these authors by writing:
Elizabeth Ludwig and Janelle Mowery
Author Relations
PO Box 721
Uhrichsville, OH 44683

A Letter to Our Readers

Dear Reader:
In order to help us satisfy your quest for more great mystery stories, we would appreciate it if you would take a few minutes to respond to the following questions. We welcome your comments and read each form and letter we receive. When completed, please return to:

Fiction Editor
Heartsong Presents—MYSTERIES!
PO Box 721
Uhrichsville, Ohio 44683

Did you enjoy reading *Where the Truth Lies* by Elizabeth Ludwig and Janelle Mowery?

Very much! I would like to see more books like this!
The one thing I particularly enjoyed about this story was:

_____
_____
_____

Moderately. I would have enjoyed it more if:

_____
_____
_____

Are you a member of the HP—MYSTERIES! Book Club?
Yes   No

If no, where did you purchase this book?

_____

Please rate the following elements using a scale of 1 (poor) to 10 (superior):

___ Main character/sleuth   ___ Romance elements

___ Inspirational theme   ___ Secondary characters

___ Setting   ___ Mystery plot

How would you rate the cover design on a scale of 1 (poor) to 5 (superior)? _____

What themes/settings would you like to see in future **Heartsong Presents—MYSTERIES!** selections? _____
_____
_____
_____

Please check your age range:
- ○ Under 18   ○ 18–24
- ○ 25–34   ○ 35–45
- ○ 46–55   ○ Over 55

Name: _____

Occupation: _____

Address: _____

E-mail address: _____

Heartsong Presents—MYSTERIES!

Any 8 Titles
for $32!
A 20%
Savings!

Great Mysteries at a Great Price! Purchase Any Title for Only $4.97 Each!

Heartsong Presents—MYSTERIES! provide romance and faith
interwoven among the pages of these fun whodunits. Written by the
talented and brightest authors in this genre, such as Christine Lynxwiler,
Cecil Murphey, Nancy Mehl, Dana Mentink, Candice Speare, and
many others, these cozy tales are sure to challenge your mind, warm your
heart, touch your spirit—and put your sleuthing skills to the test.

Not all titles may be available at time of order.
If outside the U.S., please call
740-922-7280 for shipping charges.

Along Came a Cowboy

Saddle up for a fast-paced, romantic ride. Rachel Donovan dreams of building a healing complex. The only thing standing in her way is Shady Grove's zoning laws. But by helping the town coordinate its centennial celebration, Rachel's hoping the town will, in turn, help her. Unfortunately, she keeps butting heads with Jack Westwood—a bull-headed cowboy and fellow committee member. Can Rachel fight off her unwanted attraction to this obstinate rancher while pulling off a spectacular centennial celebration?

ISBN 978-1-59789-896-6

288 Pages, $9.97

Available Wherever
Books Are Sold.